THE LIVES OF THINGS

THE LIVES OF THINGS

Short Stories

José Saramago

Translated by

Giovanni Pontiero

VERSO
London • New York

This English-language edition first published by Verso 2012

First published as *Objecto Quase*

3 5 7 9 10 8 6 4 2

Verso
UK: 6 Meard Street, London W1F 0EG
US: 20 Jay Street, Suite 1010, Brooklyn, NY 11201
www.versobooks.com

Verso is the imprint of New Left Books

ISBN-13: 978-1-84467-878-5

British Library Cataloguing in Publication Data
A catalogue record for this book is available from the British Library

Library of Congress Cataloging-in-Publication Data
Saramago, José.
[Objecto quase. English]
The lives of things : short stories / José Saramago ;
translated by Giovanni Pontiero.
p. cm.
ISBN 978-1-84467-878-5 (alk. paper)
I. Pontiero, Giovanni. II. Title.
PQ9281.A66O2513 2012
869.3'42--dc23
2011047923

Typeset in Electra by Hewer Text UK Ltd, Edinburgh
Printed in the US by Maple Vail

If man is shaped by his environment, his environment must be made human.

K. Marx and F. Engels
The Holy Family

Contents

Foreword ix

The Chair 1

Embargo 27

Reflux 45

Things 65

The Centaur 115

Revenge 139

Acknowledgements 143

Foreword

First published in 1978, this collection of six stories, originally entitled *Objecto Quase*, attests to the inventive powers of a remarkable novelist who is no less adept at mastering the techniques of shorter narrative forms. A master of suspense, he holds our attention with a subtle alternation of incisive statements and speculative digressions. Three of the stories, 'The Chair', 'Embargo' and 'Things', might be described as political allegories evoking the horror and repression which paralysed Portugal under the harsh regime of Salazar. The most powerful of these is 'The Chair', the symbol of the dictator's dramatic departure from the political scene on 6 September 1968, when the deckchair in which he was sitting collapsed and the shock precipitated a brain haemorrhage. In these narratives Saramago deploys his incomparable skill in expanding a metaphor and weaving myriad associations around the same obsessive image. With humour and compassion, he denounces the abuse of power and pays tribute to human resilience and man's will to survive in the face of injustice and institutionalised tyranny.

Here the moods vary from bitter satire and outrageous parody to Kafkaesque hallucinations when fear engenders a sense of unreality and drives a bewildered society to the brink of despair. The prevailing atmosphere in these stories is that of claustrophobia and collective hysteria. Hence the triumphant note of celebration when the fetters of censorship and prohibition are finally broken and the human spirit can breathe freely once more.

The remaining three stories in the collection provide an interesting contrast in terms of theme and tonality. And although written in a more lyrical vein, they reveal the same essential process of illumination and enhancement. The extinction of 'The Centaur' is mourned with unbearable nostalgia and pathos as the author probes the disquieting duality of this mythical creature. 'Revenge' explores the awakening desires and perceptions of adolescence with the utmost delicacy, and 'Reflux' admirably illustrates the author's instinctive sense of form and symmetry even while elaborating the most extravagant fantasies.

The one recurring theme in this collection is that of death. In these stories, however, death assumes many guises and is not necessarily physical. Nor need death imply finality. The long-awaited exit of a dictator or monarch in Saramago's fictions nearly always heralds a new era of freedom whereby ordinary men and women can emerge from nightmare and rebuild their lives.

Giovanni Pontiero
Manchester, May 1994

The Chair

The chair started to fall, to come crashing down, to topple, but not, strictly speaking, to come to bits. Strictly speaking, to come to bits means bits fall off. Now no one speaks of the chair having bits, and if it had bits, such as arms on each side, then you would refer to the arms of the chair falling off rather than coming to bits. But now that I remember, it has to be said that heavy rain comes down in buckets, so why should chairs not be able to come down in bits? At least for the sake of poetic licence? At least for the sake of being able to use an expression referred to as style? Therefore accept that chairs come to bits, although preferably they should simply fall, topple, or come crashing down. The person who does end up in pieces is the poor wretch who was sitting in this chair and is seated there no longer, but falling, as is the case, and style will exploit the variety of words which never say the same thing, however much we might want them to. If they were to say the same thing, if they were to group together through affinity of structure and origin, then life would be much simpler, by means of successive reduction, down to onomatopoeia which is not simple either, and so on and so forth, probably to silence, to what we might term the general synonym or omnivalent. It is not even onomatopoeia, or cannot be formed from this articulated sound (since the human voice does not have pure, unarticulated sounds, except perhaps in singing, and even then one would have to listen up close) formed in the throat of the person who is toppling or falling although no star, both words with heraldic echoes, which now describe anything which is about to come to pieces, therefore it did not sound right to join the parallel ending to this verb, which would settle the choice and complete the circle. Thus proving that the world is not perfect.

One could say that the chair about to topple is perfect. But times change, tastes and values change, what once seemed perfect is no longer judged to be so, for reasons beyond our control, yet which would not be reasons had times not changed. Or time. How much time need not concern us, nor need we describe or simply specify the style of furniture which would identify the chair as being one of many, especially since as a chair it naturally belongs to a simple sub-group or collateral branch, altogether different in size and function, from these sturdy patriarchs, known as tables, sideboards, wardrobes, display-cabinets for silver and crockery, or beds from which it is obviously much more difficult, if not impossible, to fall, for it is while getting out of bed that one is in danger of breaking a leg or while getting into bed that one can slip on the mat, when in fact the breaking of a leg was not precisely caused by slipping on the mat. Nor do we think it important to say from what kind of wood such a small item of furniture is made, its very name suggests it was destined to fall, unless the Latin verb *cetera* is some linguistic trap, if *cetera* is indeed Latin, as it sounds it ought to be. Any tree would have served with the exception of pine which has exhausted its properties in the making of warships and is now quite commonplace, or cherry which can easily warp, or the fig-tree which is prone to splintering, especially in hot weather or when one reaches out too far along the branch to pluck a fig; with the exception of these trees which are flawed, and others because of the many properties they possess, as in the case of ironwood which never decays yet has too much weight for the required volume. Another unsuitable wood is ebony, which is simply another name for ironwood, and we have already seen the problem of using synonyms or what are assumed to be synonyms. Not so much in this analysis of botanical matters which pays no attention to synonyms, yet scrupulously observes the two different names which different people have given to the same thing. You may be sure that the name ironwood was given or weighed up by whoever had to carry it on his back. There is no safer bet.

Were it made of ebony, we should probably have to classify the chair that is falling as being perfect, and by using verbs such as to classify or categorise, we will prevent it from falling, or only let it fall very much later, for example, a hundred years hence, when its fall would no longer be of any use to us. It is possible that another chair may topple in its place, in order to produce the same fall with a similar result, but that would mean telling a different story, not the story of what happened because it is happening, but the story of what might happen. Certainty is preferable by far, especially when you have been waiting for something far from certain.

However, we must acknowledge a degree of perfection in this singular chair which is still falling. It was not purpose-made for the body which has been sitting in it for many years but chosen instead for its design, so as to match rather than clash excessively with the other items of furniture nearby or at a distance, not made of pine, or cherry, or fig, for the reasons already stated, but of a wood commonly used for durable, high-quality furniture, for example, mahogany. This is a hypothesis which exempts us from any further verification, incidentally quite undeliberate, of the wood used to carve, mould, shape, glue, assemble, tighten up and allow to dry, this chair which is near to collapsing. So let us settle for mahogany and say no more. Except to mention how pleasant and comfortable the chair is to sit in, and if it has arms and is made entirely of mahogany, how pleasant to touch that solid and mysterious surface of smoothly polished wood, and if the arms are curved, the kind of shoulder, knee or hip-bone that curve possesses.

Mahogany, for example, unfortunately does not have the resistance of the aforementioned ebony or ironwood. The experience of men and carpenters has proved as much, and any one of us, if we can work up enough enthusiasm for these scientific matters, will be able to test this for ourselves by biting into each of these different woods and judging the difference. A normal canine tooth, however unfit to prove its strength in a circus ring, will leave a nice clear imprint on mahogany. But not on ebony. *Quod erat demonstrandum*. Whereupon we can assess the problems of rot.

There will be no police inquiry, although this might have been exactly the right moment, when the chair was tilting at a mere two degrees, since, if the whole truth be told, the sudden dislocation of the centre of gravity may be irremediable, especially when uncompensated by an instinctive reflex or force subject to that reflex; this might be the moment, I repeat, to give the order, a strict order to take everything back from this moment which cannot be postponed, not so much to the tree (or trees, for there is no guarantee that all the items of furniture come from the same planks of wood), but to the merchant, storekeeper, joiner, stevedore, shipping company responsible for shipping from remote parts the tree-trunk stripped of its branches and roots. As far back as might be necessary in order to discover where the rot first set in and what caused it. Sounds, as we know, are articulated in the throat, but they will not be capable of giving this order. They simply hesitate, as yet unaware that they are vacillating, between an exclamation and a cry, both primary. Therefore impunity is guaranteed on account of the victim's silence, and the oversight of the investigators who will simply make a routine check, once the chair has stopped falling and its collapse, not as yet fatal, has been consummated, to see whether the leg or foot has been maliciously, not to say criminally, damaged. Anyone carrying out this check will feel humiliated, for it is nothing less than humiliating to be carrying a pistol under your arm and be holding a stump of worm-eaten wood that is crumbling beneath a fingernail that need not be all that thick for this purpose. And then push the chair with the broken leg aside without showing the slightest annoyance, and then drop the leg itself, now that it has served its purpose which is precisely that of being broken.

It happened somewhere, if you will permit me this tautology. It happened somewhere that an insect of the order Coleoptera, belonging to the genus Hylotrupes, Anobium or some other genus (no entomologist has succeeded in establishing its identity) introduced itself into some part or other of the chair, from whence it then travelled, gnawing, devouring and evacuating, opening galleries along the softest veins to the ideal spot for a fracture, who knows how many years later, but ever cautious, bearing in mind the short life of the coleoptera, and how many generations must have fed on this mahogany until the day of glory, noble race, brave nation. Let us reflect on this painstaking labour, this other pyramid of Cheops, if this is how hieroglyphics are spelt, which the coleoptera built without anything showing on the outside, while opening tunnels inside which were eventually to lead into a burial chamber. There is no reason why the Pharaohs should be deposited inside mountains of stone, in some dark, mysterious place, with ramifications which first open on to abysses and perditions, where they will leave their bones and their flesh until it is devoured, however much imprudent and sceptical archaeologists may laugh at curses, the so-called Egyptologists in the former case, the experts in Lusitanian or Portuguese culture in the latter. When we come to consider the differences between the place where the pyramid is built and this other where the Pharaoh has been or is about to be installed, let us recall the wise and prudent words of our forefathers: a place for everything, and everything in its place. Therefore we need not be surprised if this pyramid called chair sometimes not only refuses its ultimate destiny, but for the duration of its fall becomes a kind of farewell, forever looking back to the beginning, not so much because of the sorrow of absence once far away, but as a perfect and convincing manifestation of what a farewell means for, as everyone knows, farewells are always much too fleeting to be truly worthy of the name. There is neither the time nor opportunity when making farewells for that sorrow ten times distilled until it becomes pure essence, nothing but confusion and panic, the tear that welled up and had no time to appear, the expression that was intended to convey deep sadness or that melancholy of another age, only to end up with a grimace or leer which is even worse. Falling like this, the chair undoubtedly falls, but all we want is the time of its falling, and as we watch this fall which nothing can stop and which none of us is likely to stop, for it is already inevitable, we can turn it back like the river Guadiana, not in fear but in bliss, which is a heavenly way of rejoicing, and once more undoubtedly deserved. With the assistance of St Teresa of Avila and the dictionary, we must try to understand that this bliss is that supernatural happiness which produces grace in the souls of the just. As we watch the chair fall, we cannot help receiving this grace, for as we stand there watching, we do nothing and will continue to do nothing to stop it from falling. Thus proving the existence of the soul because we could not possibly experience any such reaction without a soul. So let the chair go back to an upright position and recommence its fall while we get back to what we were saying.

Behold Anobium, whose name has been chosen for whatever trace of nobility it might contain, an avenger from beyond the prairie, mounted on his horse White-face, and taking his time to arrive so that all the credits can be screened and we are left in no doubt, just in case some of us missed seeing the posters in the cinema foyer about the team who made the film. Behold Anobium, now in close-up, with his coleopteral face, eaten away in its turn by the wind and the hot sun, which, as we all know, burn out the open galleries in the leg of the chair that has just broken and, thanks to which, the aforesaid chair is beginning to fall for the third time. This Anobium, as has already been stated in a form more appropriate for the banalities of genetics and reproduction, had predecessors in this act of revenge: they were called Fred, Tom Mix and Buck Jones, but these are names immortalised in the epic history of the Far West and they should not allow us to forget the anonymous coleoptera who had the much less glorious, not to say ridiculous task, of perishing while crossing the desert, or of slowly crawling through a swamp where they slipped and fell into the mire giving off the most awful stench, to hoots of laughter and catcalls from the stalls and gallery. Not one of them had settled his final account when the train gave three whistles, holsters were greased inside so that pistols could be drawn at once, with the index finger on the trigger and the thumb poised to pull back the hammer. Not one of them received the prize waiting on Mary's lips, nor was White Flash there to come from behind and push the shy cowboy into the girl's expectant arms. All pyramids have stones underneath, and the same is true of monuments. The conquering Anobium is the last in this line of anonymous heroes who preceded him, at any rate no less fortunate, for they lived, worked and died, everything in its own good time, and this Anobium, as we know, completes the cycle, and, like the male bee, he will die in the act of impregnation. The beginning of death.

Marvellous music which no one had heard for months or years, incessant, uninterrupted by day and by night, at the glorious, dazzling hour of sunrise and at this no less amazing moment when we bid the light farewell until morning, this continuous gnawing, as persistent as the endless repetition of the same note, harping on, eating away at one fibre after another and everyone entering and leaving, distractedly, absorbed in their own affairs, unaware that at the appointed hour Anobium will appear, pistol at the ready, marking out the enemy or target, taking aim which means hitting dead centre, at least that is what it means from now on, for someone had to be the first. Marvellous music, composed and played by generations of coleoptera for their pleasure and our profit, as was the destiny of the Bach family, both before and after Johann Sebastian. Music unheard, and if heard, what could it do for the person seated in this chair who will fall with it and, in fear or surprise, emit this articulated sound which may not even be a cry or shriek, much less a word. Music that will fall silent, that has fallen silent this very instant: Buck Jones sees his rival fall inexorably to the ground, beneath the harsh glare of the Texas sun, he puts his pistols away in their holsters and removes his wide-brimmed Stetson to wipe his forehead, and also because Mary, in a white dress, is running towards him, now that any danger has passed.

It would be something of an exaggeration, however, to assert that man's entire destiny is to be found inscribed in the oral chewing apparatus of the coleoptera. Were this so, we should all be living in houses made of glass and iron, and therefore be protected against Anobium, but not completely protected, because for some reason or other there is this mysterious illness which we potential victims of cancer refer to as glass cancer, and this all too common rust which, and solve who can these other mysteries, does not attack ironwood, yet literally destroys anything made simply of iron. Not only are we humans fragile, but we are even obliged to assist our own death. Perhaps it is a question of personal honour: not to be so helpless and submissive, to give something of ourselves, otherwise what is the point of being in this world? The blade of the guillotine cuts, but who offers his neck? The condemned man. The rifle-shot hits its target, but who bares his chest? The man who gets shot. Death has this strange beauty of being as lucid as a mathematical demonstration, as straightforward as drawing a line between two points, so long as it does not exceed the length of the ruler. Tom Mix fires his two pistols, but there has to be enough gunpowder pressed into the cartridges to ensure sufficient power for the bullet to cover the distance in its slightly curved trajectory (no need for a rule here), and once having met the requirements of ballistics, it has to pierce the man's cloth collar at a good height, then his shirt, which might be made of flannel, then the woollen vest that keeps him warm in winter and absorbs his sweat in summer, and finally his soft, elastic skin which initially yields, supposing, if skin supposes rather than simply suppurates, that the force of the missile will stop there and the bullets fall to the ground, into the dust on the road, and let the criminal off the hook until the next time. However, things turned out otherwise. Buck Jones is already holding Mary in his arms and the word END is coming from his mouth and about to fill the screen. Time for the spectators to rise slowly from their seats and proceed up the aisle in the direction of the harsh light coming from the exit, for they have been to the matinée, struggling to return to this humdrum reality, feeling a little sad, a little courageous, and so indifferent to the life awaiting them in the shooting gallery, that some even remain seated for the second session: once upon a time.

And now this old man is seated, having come out of one room and crossed another, then going along a passageway which could be the aisle of a cinema, but it is not, it is part of the house, not necessarily his, but simply the house in which he lives or is living, therefore not all of it is his, but in his care. The chair still has not fallen. It is condemned like a prostrate man who has not quite reached the limits of exhaustion: he can still bear his own weight. Looking at the chair from a distance, it does not appear to have been transformed by Anobium, cowboy and miner, in Arizona and Jales, in a labyrinthine network of galleries likely to make anyone lose their mind. The old man sees the chair from afar and as he gets closer, he sees, if in fact he can see the chair, that notwithstanding the thousands of times he has sat in it, he has never looked closely, and that is his mistake, now as before, never to pay attention to the chairs in which he sits because he assumes they are all capable of what only he is capable. St George would have seen the dragon there, but this old fellow is a false devotee in a skull-cap who made common cause with the cardinal patriarchs, and united, he and they, *in hoc signo vinces*. Even as he reaches the chair with a smile of innocent satisfaction, he fails to see it or notice how effectively Anobium is destroying the remaining fibres in the last gallery and is tightening the holster belt around his hips. The old man thinks he will perhaps rest for half an hour, that he might even doze a little in this pleasant autumnal weather, and that he most certainly will not have the patience to read the papers he is holding in his hand. No cause for surprise. This is not a horror film; splendid comic films have exploited and will continue to exploit similar falls, we all remember the slapstick scenes played by Chaplin or by Pat and Patachon, and there are sweets for those who can give me the titles. But let us not be hasty even though we know the chair is about to break: but not just yet, first the man has to sit down slowly, we old men are usually unsteady on our feet, we have to rest our hands or grip with force the arms or wings of the chair, to prevent our wrinkled buttocks and the seat of our pants from suddenly collapsing into the chair which has had to put up with everything, and we need not elaborate, for we are all human and know these things. We are talking about his intestines, let it be said, because this old man has many different reasons which have caused him to doubt his humanity for some considerable time. Meanwhile, he is seated like a man.

So far he has not leaned back. His weight, give or take a gramme, is equally distributed on the seat of the chair. Unless he moves, he might well sit there safely until sunset when Anobium normally recovers his strength and starts gnawing again with renewed vigour. But he is about to move, he has moved, reclining for no more than a second against the weaker side of the chair. And it breaks. First there was a crack, then when the old man shifted his weight, the leg of the chair snapped and daylight suddenly penetrated Buck Jones's gallery and lit up the target. Because of the difference between the speed of light and sounds, between the hare and the tortoise, the explosion is only heard later, dull and muffled, like the thud of a body dropping to the ground. Let us bide our time. There is no longer anyone in the parlour or bedroom, on the veranda or terrace; and while the sound of the fall goes unheard, we are the masters of this show, and we can even practise that degree of sadism, in however passive a form, which we are fortunate enough to share with the doctor or the madman, in the person who only sees and ignores or, from the outset, rejects any obligation even if only humanitarian to render any help. Certainly not to this old man.

He is about to fall backwards. There he goes. Here, right in front of him, the chosen spot, we observe that he has a long face and an aquiline nose, sharp as a hook cum knife, and were it not for the fact that he has suddenly opened his mouth, we would be entitled, like any eye-witness who can say I saw him with my own eyes, to swear that he has no lips. But his mouth has opened, opens in surprise, alarm and bewilderment, making it possible to perceive, however indistinctly, two folds of flesh as colourless as larvae, which only because of the difference in dermal texture are not to be confused with the surrounding pallor. His double chin trembles over the larynx and other cartilages, and his whole body accompanies the chair backwards, while on the floor the broken leg has rolled over to one side, not far away, because we are there to look on. It has scattered a dense, yellow dust, not all that much, but enough for us to delight in the image of an hour-glass with sand that consists eschatologically of the excrement of coleoptera: which goes to show just how absurd it would be to put Buck Jones and his horse White-face here, that is assuming that Buck changed horses at the last hostelry and is now riding Fred's horse. But let us forget this dust which is not even sulphur, and would greatly enhance the scene if it were, burning with a bluish flame and giving off the foul stench of sulphuric acid. Such a sonorous phrase! And what an excellent way of conjuring up hell in all its horror, as Beelzebub's chair breaks and falls backwards, taking with it Satan, Asmodeus and his legion.

The old man is no longer gripping the arms of the chair, his knees have suddenly stopped trembling and are now obeying the other law, and his feet which were always clad in boots to disguise the fact that they were cloven (no one read with sufficient haste or attention, it is all there, the goat's cloven hoof), his feet are already in the air. We shall watch this impressive gymnastic feat, the back somersault, the latter much more spectacular, despite the absence of an audience, than those others seen in stadiums and arenas, from some lofty tribune, at a time when chairs were still solid and Anobium an improbable hypothesis of labour. And there is no one to fix this moment. My kingdom for a polaroid, shouted Richard III, and no one paid any heed, for his request was much too premature. The nothing we possess in exchange for this everything of showing a photograph of our children, our membership card and a faithful image of the fall. Ah, those feet in the air, ever further from the ground, ah, that head ever closer, ah, Santa Comba, not the saint of the afflicted, but rather the patron saint of that which ever afflicted them. The daughters of Mondego do not as yet lament obscure death. This fall is not any old Chaplin stunt, it is impossible to repeat, it is unique and, therefore, as excellent as when Adam's accomplishments were linked with the graces of Eve. And speaking of Eve, domestic and servile, and demanding whenever necessary, benefactress of the unemployed if they are frugal, honest and catholic, such martyrdom, soaring and souring power in the shadow of this Adam who falls without apple or serpent, where are you? You have spent far too much time in the kitchen, or on the telephone listening to the Daughters of Mary or the Handmaidens of the Sacred Heart, or the Children of St Zita, you are wasting far too much water on those potted begonias, much too easily distracted, a queen bee who never comes when summoned, and if you were to come to whom would you render assistance? It is late. The saints have turned away, they whistle, pretend not to notice, for they know very well that there are no miracles, there never have been, and that whenever something extraordinary happened in the world, it was their good fortune to be present and to take advantage. Not even St Joseph, who in his time was a carpenter, and a better carpenter than a saint, could have glued that wooden leg in time to avoid its collapse, before this latest Portuguese champion gymnast made a somersault, and domestic Eve who looks after the house is even now sorting out the bottles of pills and drops the old man must take, one at a time, before, during and after his next meal.

The old man notices the ceiling. He merely notices it but has no time to look. He moves his arms and legs like an upturned turtle with its belly in the air, before looking more like a seminarian in boots masturbating at home during the holidays while his parents are out harvesting. Just this and nothing more. Simple earth, sweet and rough for one to tread and then say that it is nothing but stones, that we are born poor and fortunately we shall die poor, and that is why we are in God's grace. Fall, old man, fall. See how your feet are higher than your head. Before making your somersault, Olympic medallist, you will reach the zenith that boy on the beach failed to reach for he tried and fell, with only one arm because he had left the other behind in Africa. Fall. But not too quickly: there is still plenty of sunshine in the sky. We spectators can actually go up to a window and look out at our leisure, and from there have a grand view of towns and villages, of rivers and plains, of hills and dales, and tell scheming Satan that this is the world we want, for there is no harm in wanting what is rightfully ours. With startled eyes we go back inside and it is as if you were not there: we have brought too much sunshine into the room and we must wait until it gets used to the place or goes back outside. You are now much closer to the ground. The good leg and damaged leg of the chair have already slid forward, all sense of balance gone. The real fall is clearly imminent, the surrounding atmosphere has become distorted, objects cower in terror, they are under attack, their whole body twisting and twitching, like a cat with rheumatism, therefore incapable of giving that last spin in the air that would bring salvation, its four paws on the ground and the quiet thud of an all too live animal. It is obvious just how badly this chair was placed, unaware of Anobium's presence and the damage he was doing inside: worse, in fact, or just as bad as that edge, tip or corner of a piece of furniture extending its clenched fist to some point in space, for the time being still free, still unperturbed and innocent, where the curve of the circle formed by the old man's head is about to be interrupted and stand out, change direction for a second and then fall once more, downwards, to the bottom, inexorably drawn by that sprite at the centre of the universe who has billions of tiny strings in his hand, which he pulls up and down, like a puppeteer here on earth, until one last tug removes us from the stage. That moment has still not come for the old man, but he is already falling in order to fall again for the last time. And now that there is space, what space remains between the corner of the piece of furniture, the clenched fist, the lance in Africa, and the more fragile side of the head, the predestined bone? If we measure it we will be shocked at the tiny amount of space there is to cover, look, not even enough space for a finger, much less a fingernail, a shaving-blade, a hair, a simple thread spun by a silkworm or spider. There is still some time left, but soon there will be no more space. The spider has just expelled its last filament, is putting the finishing touch to its cocoon, the fly already trapped.

This sound is curious. Clear, somehow clear, so as not to leave those of us present in any doubt, yet muffled, dull, discreet, so that domesticated Eve and the Cains of this world do not arrive too soon, so that everything may take place between what is alone and solitary as befits such greatness. His head, as foreseen and in accordance with the laws of physics, hit the ground before bouncing a little, let me say about two centimetres up and to one side; now that we are at the scene and have taken other measurements. From now on the chair no longer matters. Not even the rest of the fall is of any further consequence for it is now irrelevant. Buck Jones's plan included, as we have already mentioned, a trajectory, it had a goal in mind. There it is.

Whatever may happen now is on the inside. First let it be said, however, that the body fell again, and the accompanying chair, of which no more will be said or only in passing. It is indifferent to the fact that the speed of sound should suddenly equal the speed of light. What had to be, happened. Eve might frantically rush to help, muttering prayers as one does on these occasions, or perhaps not on this occasion, if it is true that catastrophes leave their victims speechless, although they can still scream. Which explains why domesticated Eve, such martyrdom, kneels and asks questions now that the catastrophe is over and all that remains are the consequences. It will not be long before the Cains appear from everywhere if it is not unfair to call them by the name of the wretched fellow on whom the Lord turned his back, thereby taking human revenge on an obsequious and scheming brother. Nor shall we call them vultures, even though they move like this, or don't, or do:

much more accurate under the dual heading of morphology and characterology, to include them in the chapter of hyenas, and this is a great discovery. With the important exception that hyenas, just like vultures, are useful animals who clear dead flesh from the landscapes of the living, and for this we should be grateful to them, while they continue to be the hyena and its own dead flesh, and this, in the final analysis, is the great discovery we mentioned earlier. The perpetuum mobile, contrary to what amateur inventors and enlightened wonder-workers of carpentry ingenuously imagine, is not mechanical. Rather it is biological, it is this hyena feeding on its dead and putrefied body, thereby constantly reconstituting itself in death and putrefaction. To interrupt the cycle, not everything would suffice, yet the slightest thing would be ample. At times, were Buck Jones not away on the other side of the mountain in pursuit of some simple and honest cattle-rustlers, a chair would serve, both as a fulcrum to lever the earth, as Archimedes said to Heron of Syracuse, and to burst the blood vessels which the bones of the cranium judged they were protecting, and judged is used here literally, for it seemed unlikely that bones so near to the brain could be incapable of carrying out, by means of osmosis or symbiosis, a mental operation as simple as passing judgment. And even so, should this cycle be interrupted, we must pay attention to what might graft itself on at the moment of rupture, for it could turn out to be, not through grafting this time, another hyena emerging from that festering flank, like Mercury from Jupiter's thigh, if I might be permitted this comparison with ancient mythology. But that is another story which has probably been told before.

Domesticated Eve ran from this place, calling out and uttering words not worth repeating, so similar as to make little difference, although scarcely mediaeval, to those spoken by Leonor Teles when they murdered Andeiro, and, besides, she was a queen. This old man is not dead. He has simply fainted, and we can sit cross-legged on the floor at our ease, for a second is a century, and before the doctors and stretcher-bearers and hyenas in striped trousers arrive weeping their eyes out, an eternity will have passed. Let us take a closer look. Deathly pale, but not cold. His heart is beating, his pulse steady, the old man appears to be asleep, and I'll be damned if this has not been one great blunder, a monstrous ruse to separate good from evil, wheat from the chaff, friends from foes, those in favour from those who are opposed, given the part played by that raffish and disreputable trouble-maker Buck Jones in this whole business about the chair.

Now then, you Portuguese, calm down and listen patiently. As you know, the skull consists of the bones enclosing the brain, which in its turn, as we can see from this anatomical chart in natural colours, is nothing less than the upper part of the spinal cord. Compressed all the way down the back, it found a space there and opened out like a flower of intelligence. Note that the comparison is neither gratuitous nor disparaging. There is an enormous variety of flowers, and we need only remember, or let each of us remember the one we like best, and in the last resort, for example, the one we dislike most, a carnivorous flower, *de gustibus et coloribus non est disputandum*, assuming we share this horror of anything that denatures itself, although in keeping with that basic rigour demanded of those who teach and learn, we ought to question the justice of this accusation, and although, once more so that nothing is overlooked, we should ask ourselves what right a plant has got to nourish itself twice, first on the soil and then on whatever is flying through the air in the multiple form of insects, or even birds. Let us note in passing how easy it is to suspend judgement, to receive information from all sides, accept them at face value, and remain neutral on the grounds that we are an undivided spirit, and offer daily sacrifice at the altar of prudence, our best fornication. We were not neutral, however, as we watched that fall in slow motion. And a degree of prudence has to be sacrificed if we are to accompany, with due attention, the movement of the pointer passing over this incision in the brain.

Observe, ladies and gentlemen, this longitudinal bridge, as it were, made from fibres: it is called the fornix and constitutes the upper part of the optic thalamus. Behind can be seen two transversal commissures which obviously are not to be confused with those of the lips. Now let us examine the other side. Look here. What you see standing out are the quadrigeminal tubercles or optic lobes (and since this is not a Zoology lesson, the accent on lobes is heavily stressed on the o). This broad section is the anterior brain, and here we have the famous convolutions. Right underneath, as everyone knows, is the cerebellum which contains what is known as the arbor vitae, and in case anyone mistakes this for a Botany lesson, we should explain that this is due to the plicae of nervous tissue in a certain number of lamellae, which in their turn produce secondary folds. We mentioned the spinal cord earlier. Take a good look at this. It is not a bridge yet is known as the bridge of Varolio, which sounds more like the name of an Italian town, and I defy you to disagree. Behind is the elongated medulla. I have almost finished this description, so bear with me. Much more could be explained and in greater detail, but only if we were carrying out an autopsy. Therefore let us simply point out the pituitary gland, a glandular and nervous organ at the base of the thalamus or third ventricle. And to conclude, let me point out the optic nerve, a subject of the greatest importance, and now no one can claim not to have witnessed what happened in this place.

And now to the crucial question: what purpose does the brain, or brains as they are commonly known, serve? They serve for everything because they allow us to think. But we must be careful not to be deceived by the common misconception that everything inside the skull is related to thought and the senses. An unforgivable error, ladies and gentlemen. The greater part of this mass inside the cranium has nothing to do with thought and does not influence it in any way. Only the thinnest layer of nervous tissue, known as the cortex, about three millimetres thick, and covering the anterior part of the brain, constitutes the seat of consciousness. Please note the disconcerting similarity between what we define as the microcosm and what we shall refer to as the macrocosm, between the three millimetres of cortex which allow us to think and the few kilometres of atmosphere which permit us to breathe, each and every one of them insignificant in their turn, not just when compared with the size of the galaxy, but even the simple diameter of the earth. Let us walk in awe, dear brethren, and pray to the Lord.

The body is still here, and will remain here for as long as we wish. Here, where the hair looks dishevelled, is the spot where his head struck the ground. To all appearances, it is nothing serious. The faintest bruise, as if scratched by an impatient fingernail and virtually covered by a root of hair so that one would never suspect death might enter here. In fact, it is already inside. What is this? Are we to take pity on our vanquished enemy? Is death an excuse, a pardon, a sponge, a lye for washing away crimes? The old man has now opened his eyes but fails to recognise us, for he does not know us. His chin trembles, he tries to speak, is disturbed by our presence here, and believes we are responsible for this outrage. He says nothing. Saliva trickles from his gaping mouth down on to his chin. What would Sister Lucia do in this case, what would she do if she were here on her knees, enshrouded in the triple odour of mustiness, petticoats and incense? Would she reverently wipe away the saliva or, with even greater reverence, prostrate herself, using her tongue to gather that holy secretion, that relic, to be preserved in an ampoule? Neither the annals of the church nor, as we know, the history books will say, and not even domesticated Eve will notice, afflicted soul, the outrage the old man is committing by slobbering over himself.

Steps can already be heard in the passage-way, but there is still time. The bruise has turned darker and the hair covering it appears to be bristling. A gentle combing would suffice to tidy up this patch. But to no avail. On another surface, that of the cortex, the blood gathers as it pours from the vessels the blow divided into sections at the precise spot where the fall occurred. A case of haematoma. It is there that Anobium is to be found at this moment, ready for the second shift. Buck Jones has cleaned his revolver and is reloading the barrel with fresh bullets. He is already on his way to look for the old man. That scratching of nails, that hysterical wailing, the laughter of hyenas, with which we are all familiar. Let us go to the window. What do you think of this month of September? We have not had such weather in a long time.

Embargo

He awoke with the distinct feeling of having been interrupted in the middle of a dream and saw before him the grey and frosty window-pane, the square, livid eye of dawn upon him, cut in the shape of a cross and dripping with condensation. He thought his wife must have forgotten to draw the curtains before going to bed, and felt irritated: unless he could get back to sleep, his day would be ruined. But he had no intention of getting up to draw the curtains: he preferred to cover his face with the sheet and turn to his wife, who was asleep, to take refuge in her warmth and in the perfume of her dishevelled hair. He waited a few more minutes, ill at ease, fearful at the morning insomnia. But then he consoled himself with the thought that bed was such a warm cocoon and with the labyrinthine presence of the body pressed against his and, almost slipping into a slow spiral of erotic images, he went back to sleep. The grey eye of the window-pane gradually turned blue, staring all the while at the two heads resting on the pillow like the forgotten remains of a removal to some other house or some other world. When the alarm went off two hours later, daylight filled the room.

He told his wife not to get up, to stay in bed a little longer, while he slipped out into the chilly atmosphere with that unmistakable sense of dampness on the walls, the door-knobs, the bath-towels. He smoked his first cigarette as he shaved and the second with his coffee which had cooled in the meantime. He coughed, as he did every morning. Then, groping for his clothes, he dressed without switching on the light. He was anxious not to awaken his wife. The refreshing fragrance of eau de Cologne enlivened the shadows, causing his wife to sigh with pleasure when her husband leaned over the bed to kiss her closed eyes. And he whispered that he would not be coming home for lunch.

He closed the door and quickly went downstairs. The building seemed quieter than usual. Perhaps because of the mist, he thought. For he had noticed that the mist was like a bell-jar, muffling sounds and transforming them, breaking them up, doing to them what it did to images. It had to be the mist. On the last flight of stairs he could already see the street and confirm whether he had been right. After all, the light was still grey, but as harsh and bright as crystal. On the edge of the pavement lay an enormous dead rat. And standing there at the door, he was lighting his third cigarette when a boy with a cap pulled over his head went past and spat on the animal, as he himself had been taught and had always seen others do.

His car was five blocks down the road. What a stroke of luck to have found a parking space. He clung to the superstition that the further away he parked the car at night, the greater the risk of having it stolen. Without ever having actually said so, he was convinced that he would never see his car again if he were to leave it in some remote part of the city. Having it there nearby gave him greater reassurance. The car appeared to be covered with tiny drops of moisture, the windows covered in condensation. Were it not quite so cold, you would have thought the car was perspiring like a human body. He examined the tyres as usual, checked in passing that the aerial was not broken and opened the door. Inside the car, the air was freezing cold. With its windows clouded, the car resembled a transparent cavern submerged by a deluge of water. He decided it would have been better to have parked on a slope in order to drive off more easily. He switched on the ignition and at the same instant the engine rumbled with a deep, impatient panting. He smiled, pleasantly surprised. The day was getting off to a good start.

The car sped up the street, scraping the asphalt like an animal with its hooves, pounding the rubbish scattered around. The speedometer suddenly leapt to ninety, a suicidal speed in such a narrow street with cars parked on both sides. What was happening? Alarmed, he took his foot off the accelerator. For a moment he thought they must have given him a much more powerful engine. He put his foot down cautiously on the accelerator and brought the car under control. Nothing serious. Sometimes you can misjudge the pressure of your foot on the pedal. The heel of your shoe only has to come down in the wrong place to alter the movement and pressure. So easily done.

Distracted by this incident, he still had not checked the petrol gauge. Could someone have stolen his petrol during the night as had happened before? No. The pointer indicated that the tank was exactly half-full. He stopped at a red light, feeling the car vibrate and tense up as he held the wheel. Strange. He had never noticed this animal-like shudder running in waves through the bodywork and churning his insides. When the light turned green, the car appeared to snake, to become elongated like fluid, in order to overtake the cars in front. Strange. But then he had always considered himself a better than average driver. A question of having the right temperament, these quick reflexes which were probably exceptional. The tank half-full. If he should come across a petrol station that was open, he would fill up the tank. Considering the number of rounds he would have to make today before going to the office, better to play safe and have petrol in reserve. This absurd embargo. The panic, the hours of waiting, the endless queues of cars. Industry would almost certainly suffer the consequences. The tank half-full. Other motorists driving around with even less petrol, but if only you could prove it. The car took a sharp bend before climbing up a steep slope without the slightest effort. Nearby was a petrol-pump few people knew existed and he might be lucky. Like a setter following the scent the car dodged in and out of the traffic, turned two corners and took its place in the queue. What a good idea.

He looked at his watch. There must have been about twenty cars in front of him. Could be worse. But he decided it might be wiser to go to the office first and leave his rounds until the afternoon, when he would have a full tank of petrol and nothing more to worry about. He lowered the window and hailed a passing newsvendor. The weather had turned much colder. But there, inside the car, with the newspaper spread over the wheel, smoking while he waited, he felt a pleasant warmth as if he were back between the sheets. He stretched his back muscles with the voluptuous contortions of a cat at the thought of his wife still snuggled up in bed at that hour, and reclined more comfortably in his seat. The newspaper had nothing good to report. The embargo continued. A cold, gloomy Christmas, read one of the headlines. But he still had half a tank of petrol and it would not be long before it was full. The car in front edged forward a little. Good.

After an hour and a half he found himself at the head of the queue, and three minutes later he was driving off. A little worried because the pump-attendant had told him, without any particular expression in his voice after repeating the information so often, that there would be no more petrol for a fortnight. On the seat beside him, the newspaper announced severe restrictions. Never mind, at least his tank was full. What should he do? Go straight to the office or first call at a client's house and see if he could pick up an order. He opted for the client. It was preferable to justify his lateness with a business call rather than say that he had spent an hour and a half queuing for petrol when he still had the tank half-full. The car was doing fine. He had never felt happier driving it. He switched on the radio and caught the news. Things were going from bad to worse. These Arabs. This ridiculous embargo. Suddenly the car gave a lurch and veered towards the road to the right before coming to a halt in a queue of cars smaller than the first one. What had gone wrong? He had a full tank, well, practically full, damn it. He manipulated the gear lever and tried to reverse, but the gear-box refused to obey him. He tried forcing it, but the gears seemed to be blocked. How ludicrous. That something should go wrong now. The car in front advanced. Expecting the worst, he cautiously went into first gear. No problem. He sighed with relief. But how would the reverse gear react when he had to use it again?

About thirty minutes later he was putting a half-litre of petrol in the tank and feeling foolish beneath the disdainful look of the pump-attendant. He gave him an absurdly big tip and drove off with a screeching of tyres and acceleration. How preposterous. Now for his client otherwise the morning would be lost. The car was running better than ever. It responded to his movements as if it were a mechanical extension of his own body. But this business about reversing bothered him. And now he really did have cause for concern. An enormous lorry had broken down and was blocking the entire street. There had not been enough time to get round it and now he was stuck. Once again he anxiously manipulated the lever and the car went into reverse gear with a gentle sound of suction. He could not recall the gear-box ever having reacted in this way before. He turned the steering wheel to the left, accelerated, and with one spurt, the car mounted the pavement, went right up against the lorry, and came out on the other side, as free and agile as an animal on the loose. The damned car had nine lives. Perhaps because of all the upheaval caused by the embargo, with everyone in a panic and services disrupted, the pumps had been filled with a much higher grade of petrol. That would be fun.

He looked at his watch. Was it worth calling on his client? With luck, he would get there before they closed. If the traffic was not too heavy he would have enough time. But the traffic was heavy. Christmas time, and notwithstanding the shortage of petrol, everyone out on the roads, making life difficult for those who had to get to work. And on coming to a crossroads that was clear, he turned off and decided not to visit his client after all. Better to make some excuse in the office and postpone the call until the afternoon. With so much hesitation, he had made quite a detour from the centre. All that petrol consumed for nothing. But then the tank was full. As he drove down a street he saw more cars queuing in the square below. He smiled with satisfaction and accelerated, determined to sound his hooter as he passed those paralysed motorists who were waiting. But twenty metres further on his car veered to the left by itself and came to a halt at the end of the queue with a gentle sigh. What was happening? He had not intended to queue for petrol. Why had the car stopped when the tank was full? He studied the various dials, checked the steering wheel as if unfamiliar with his own car and, with one further gesture, he pulled the rear-view mirror towards him and looked at his reflection. He could see that he was worried and with good reason. Once again in the rear-view mirror he could see a car coming down the road and clearly heading for the queue. Worried about being trapped there, when his tank was full, he quickly manoeuvred the lever to go backwards. The car resisted and the lever slipped from his grasp. He instantly found himself jammed between his two neighbours. Damn it. What could be wrong with the car? He must take it to the garage. A reverse gear that works one minute but not the next is a real hazard.

More than twenty minutes passed before he reached the pump. He saw the attendant approach and his voice faltered as he asked him to check the tank. At the same time he tried to get out of this embarrassing situation, quickly putting the car into first gear and trying to drive off. To no avail. The pump-attendant looked at him suspiciously, opened the tank and, after a few seconds, came and charged him for a litre, muttering to himself as he pocketed the money. Next moment the car went into first gear without any effort and advanced, moving smoothly with a low purr. There had to be something not quite right with the car, the gear changes, the engine, something somewhere, damn it. Or could he be losing his touch as a driver? Or even be ill? He had slept so well, had no more worries than usual. Better to forget his clients for the moment, not think about them for the rest of the day and remain in the office. He felt restless. The bodywork of the car was shaking all over, not on the surface but inside the steel parts, and the engine was running with that inaudible sound of lungs breathing in and out, in and out. To his dismay he began to realise that he was mentally tracing out an itinerary that would take him far away from other petrol-pumps, and this was enough to make him apprehensive and fear for his sanity. He started going round in circles, lengthening and shortening the journey, until he arrived in front of his office. He found a parking space and sighed with relief. After switching off the engine, he removed the key and opened the door. But he could not get out.

He thought he had caught the hem of his raincoat, that his leg had got stuck round the column of the steering wheel, and he tried another movement. He even checked the safety belt to see whether he had put it on without noticing. No. The belt was hanging at his side, a soft, black intestine. How absurd, he thought. I must be ill. If I cannot get out, it's because I am ill. He could move his arms and legs without any difficulty and bend his trunk with each manoeuvre, look back, lean slightly to the right, towards the glove-box, but his back was attached to his seat. Not firmly, but rather as a limb is attached to the body. He lit a cigarette, and suddenly felt worried about what his boss might say if he were to peer through the window and see him sitting there smoking inside the car and in no hurry to get out. A loud hoot made him close the door he had opened on to the road. When the other car had passed, he slowly opened the door again, threw out his cigarette and, clutching the steering-wheel with both hands, made a brusque and violent movement. Useless. He did not even feel any pain. The back of the seat held him comfortably and kept him there. What on earth was happening? He pulled the rear-view mirror downwards and looked at himself. No visible difference in his expression. Except for a vague anxiety he could barely control. On turning his head towards the pavement on the right, he saw a little girl staring at him, at once intrigued and amused. Then a woman appeared with an overcoat which the little girl slipped into without averting her gaze. And as they walked away the mother began arranging the girl's collar and hair.

He took another look in the mirror and understood what he must do. But not there. People were watching, some of them acquaintances. He straightened up the car, hastily reaching out for the handle to close the door, and then sped down the street as fast as possible. He had a goal, a clearly defined objective which made him feel more tranquil, so much so that he allowed himself to smile which gradually alleviated his anguish.

He had almost passed the petrol-pump before he noticed it. There was a placard announcing 'Out of Petrol', and the car moved on without the slightest detour or reducing its speed. He did not want to think about the car. He was smiling again. Leaving the city behind, he reached the suburbs, close to the place he was looking for. He entered a road that was under construction, turned left, then right, until he came to a deserted narrow track with a ditch on either side. It was starting to rain when he stopped the car.

His idea was simple. All he had to do was to get out of his raincoat by wriggling his arms and body, then slither out like a snake shedding its skin. In the presence of other people he would never have the courage, but there, all alone, with wilderness all around him, and the city remote and hidden by the rain, nothing would be easier. But he was mistaken. Not only was his raincoat stuck to the back of his seat, but also his jacket, his sweater, his shirt, his vest, his skin, his muscles and bones. This is what he was unconsciously thinking ten minutes later as he twisted and turned inside the car, calling out and close to tears. Desperate. He was imprisoned in the car. However much he struggled to get out through the open door where the rain was being driven in by sudden icy gusts of wind, however much he pressed his feet against the protruding speedometer, he could not pull himself out of his seat. Using both hands he held on to the roof and tried to hoist himself up. He might just as well have been trying to lift the universe. He threw himself over the wheel, howling and terrified out of his wits. Before his eyes, the windscreen wipers, which he had involuntarily set in motion in his agitation, went back and forth with the dry sound of a metronome. From afar came the noise of a factory siren. Next moment a man riding a bicycle came round the bend, his head and shoulders covered with a large sheet of black plastic, the rain trickling down as if it were sealskin. The cyclist looked inquisitively inside the car and pedalled on, perhaps disappointed or intrigued to see a man on his own and not a couple, as he had surmised from a distance.

What was happening was preposterous. No one had ever been imprisoned like this inside his own car, by his own car. There must be some way or other of getting out. Certainly not by force. Perhaps in a garage. But how would he explain it? Should he call the police? And then what? People would gather round, everyone staring, while an officer grabbed him by an arm and asked those present to help him, but in vain, because the back of the seat was gently clasping him in its embrace. Journalists and photographers would soon rush to the scene and photographs would appear in all the newspapers next day, showing him trapped inside his car and looking as mortified as a shorn animal out in the rain. There had to be another solution. He switched off the engine and without interrupting the gesture threw himself violently outwards as if launching a surprise attack. With no result. He knocked his head and his left hand and the pain made him feel quite dizzy, while a sudden and uncontrollable desire to urinate released an endless flow of warm liquid that ran down between his legs on to the floor of the car. No sooner did he feel this happening than he began to sob quietly, moaning in his misery, and there he remained until a mangy dog emerged from the rain and came up to the car door to bark at him without much conviction.

He slowly went into gear with the heavy movements of some subterranean nightmare and proceeded along the narrow track trying hard not to think, not to allow the situation to prey on his mind. He was vaguely aware that he must find someone to help him. But who? He was reluctant to alarm his wife, but what else could he do. Perhaps she might be able to come up with a solution. At least he would not feel so wretchedly alone.

He drove back into the city, observing the traffic signals and moving as little as possible in his seat, as if anxious to appease the powers holding him there. Several hours went by and the light was fading. He saw three petrol-pumps but the car did not react. All three displayed a placard announcing: 'Out of Petrol'. Once he entered the city he began to see cars abandoned in the oddest places and displaying red triangles in the back window, a sign which on other occasions would have meant a breakdown, but which now nearly always meant out of petrol. Twice he came across groups of men pushing vehicles on to the pavements, with wild gestures of exasperation beneath the rain which was still falling.

When he finally reached the street where he lived he had to think how he could summon his wife. He stopped the car in front of the door, disorientated, almost on the brink of another nervous crisis. He waited for the miracle to happen whereby his wife would come down in answer to his silent plea for help. He waited for some time before an inquisitive lad from the neighbourhood approached whom he was able to persuade with the promise of a reward to go up to the third floor and tell the lady who lived there that her husband was waiting below in the car. That she should come at once for it was very urgent.

The boy went and came down again, said the lady was coming and ran off having earned his reward.

His wife came down in her house attire, having forgotten even to bring an umbrella, and now she was standing there in the doorway, undecided, involuntarily turning her eyes towards a dead rat at the edge of the pavement, a limp rat with bristling hairs; hesitant about crossing the pavement in the rain, somewhat annoyed with her husband who had made her come down needlessly when he could so easily have come up himself to tell her what he wanted. But when she saw her husband gesticulating inside the car, she took fright and ran to him. She reached out for the door-handle, anxious to escape the rain, and when she finally opened the door, she confronted her husband's open hand pushing her away without actually touching her. She persisted and tried to get in but he shouted that she must not, that it was dangerous, and he explained what was happening as she leaned over, getting all the rain on her back and bare head, her whole face twitching with horror. And she watched her husband in that warm and misted cocoon isolating him from the world, writhing in his seat as he struggled unsuccessfully to get out of the car. She grabbed him by the arm and pulled in disbelief, unable to budge him an inch. And since it was all too horrible to contemplate, they remained there staring at each other in silence until she thought her husband must be mad and was pretending not to be able to get out. She must go and fetch someone to help him, to take him wherever such mental disorders are treated. In soothing tones she told her husband to be patient while she went to fetch someone to help her release him, she would not be long, they would even be able to lunch together and he could ring the office and say he had flu. And therefore he would not need to go to work that afternoon. He must remain calm, there was nothing to worry about, it would not be long now until he was free.

But when she disappeared upstairs, he once more imagined himself surrounded by onlookers, his photograph in the papers, the mortification of having peed down his legs, and he waited a few more minutes. And while his wife was upstairs making telephone calls everywhere, to the police, to the hospital, trying to persuade them to believe her and not to be taken in by the natural tone of voice in which she gave her name and that of her husband, the colour of the vehicle, the make and registration number, he could no longer bear to wait and switched on the engine. When his wife came back downstairs, the car had gone and the rat had finally slipped off the edge of the pavement and was rolling down the sloping road, carried off by the water running from the gutters. The woman called out, but it was some time before anyone appeared, and how was she to explain what had happened?

Until darkness fell the man drove around the city, passing empty petrol-pumps, finding himself in queues quite unintentionally, worried because his money was running out and he did not like to think what would happen once he had no money left and the car stopped in front of a petrol-pump to fill up with more petrol. But no such thing happened for the simple reason that nearly all the pumps were closing and any remaining queues were waiting for them to re-open next morning, and so the best solution was to avoid any pump that might still be working so as not to have to stop. On a long, broad avenue with very little traffic, a police car accelerated and overtook him, and as it passed him, the policeman waved him down. But once again he lost his nerve and drove on. He could hear the police siren behind him and also saw, coming from who knows where, a motorcyclist in uniform who was almost on his tail. But the car, his car, sped away with one almighty roar and headed for the access to the motorway. The police followed him at a distance, ever further away, and by nightfall there was no longer any sign of them and his car was speeding along another road.

He was feeling hungry. He had peed again, much too humiliated to feel any shame. And he was a little delirious: humiliated, homiliated. He went on declining, altering the consonants and syllables in an unconscious and obsessive exercise which shielded him from reality. He did not stop because he did not know what he should stop for. But in the early hours of morning he parked the car on several occasions at the side of the road and tried to ease himself out ever so slowly, as if in the meantime he and the car had made a truce and this was the moment to put their goodwill to the test. Twice he spoke in a low voice when the seat held on to him, twice he tried to coax the car to release him, twice in that freezing and nocturnal wilderness, where the rain never ceased, he broke down, wailing and weeping in blind despair. The open wounds on his head and hand began bleeding again. While he, sobbing his heart out and whining like a frightened animal, went on driving the car. Allowing himself to be driven.

He travelled all night without knowing where he was going. He passed through villages unknown to him, covered long, straight roads, went up and down mountain slopes, circled curves and bends, and as dawn broke, he was somewhere on an old road where the rain had formed puddles rippling on the surface. The engine rumbled furiously as it dragged its wheels through the mud, and the whole car was vibrating and making the most alarming noises. Morning came without any sign of the sun appearing but the rain suddenly stopped. The road became a simple track which, further ahead, constantly gave the impression of losing itself amidst boulders. Where had the world gone? Before him he saw mountains and an ominously low sky. He screamed and beat on the wheel with clenched fists. Just then he saw that the indicator was pointing to zero. The engine appeared to be starting up by itself and dragged the car another twenty metres. Beyond, he could see the paved road again but he had used up all his petrol.

A cold sweat broke out on his forehead. Overcome with nausea, he could feel a veil being drawn over his eyes three times. Groping, he opened the door to prevent himself from suffocating and, at that moment, either because he was dying or the engine had gone dead, his body slumped to the left and slid out of the car. It slipped a little further and ended up lying on the road. The rain had started again.

Reflux

First of all, since everything must have a beginning, even if that beginning is the final point from which it cannot be separated, and to say cannot is not to say wishes not, or must not, it is simply impossible, for if such a separation were feasible, we all know that the entire universe would collapse, inasmuch as the universe is a fragile construction incapable of withstanding permanent solutions – first of all, the four routes were opened up. Four wide roads divided the country, starting from their cardinal points in a straight line or ever so slightly bent to follow the earth's curvature, and therefore as rigorously as possible tunnelling through mountains, dividing plains, and overcoming, supported on pillars, passing over rivers and valleys. Five kilometres from the place where they would intersect, if this were the builders' intention or rather the order received from the royal personage at the appropriate moment, the roads divided off into a network of major and secondary routes, like enormous arteries which had to transform themselves into veins and capillaries in order to proceed, and this self-same network found itself confined within a perfect square which clearly measured ten kilometres on each side. This square which also had started out, bearing in mind the universal observation that opened the story, as four rows of trig points set out on the ground, subsequently became – once the machines that opened, levelled and paved the four roads appeared on the horizon, coming, as we said, from the four cardinal points – subsequently became a high wall, four curtain-walls which could soon be seen, as was already clear from the drawing-boards, delimiting a hundred square kilometres of flat or levelled ground, because a certain amount of clearing had to be done. Land chosen to meet the basic need of equidistance from that place to the frontiers, a relative advantage, which was fortunately confirmed later by a high lime content which not even the most optimistic had the courage to forecast in their plans when asked for their opinion: all of this simply brought greater glory to the royal personage, as might have been predicted from the outset if greater attention had been paid to the dynasty's history: all its monarchs had always been right, and others less so, according to the accounts of events which were officially recorded. Such a project could never have been carried out without a strong will and the money that permits one to have a will and the hope of seeing it fulfilled, the reason why the nation's coffers paid for this gigantic enterprise on a per capita basis, which naturally meant levying a general tax on the entire population, not according to income but in the inverse order of life expectancy, since this was considered to be just and readily understood by everyone: the older the person, the higher the tax.

There were some remarkable feats in carrying out a project of this magnitude; endless problems arose, and workers who had been sent ahead met their death even before the cemetery was finished, many were buried in a landslide, some fell from great heights, calling out in vain, others were struck down by sunstroke, or suddenly froze on the spot, lymph, urine and blood having turned to cold stone. All of them victims of being in the vanguard. But the accolade of genius, provisional immortality, excepting that inherent in the King which was guaranteed to last longer, was bestowed by luck and merit on the discreet civil servant who argued that the gates in the walls on the original plan were unnecessary. He was right. It would have been absurd to make and install gates which had to remain open at all hours of day and night. Thanks to this diligent civil servant, some savings were made: the money it would have cost to make four main gates and sixteen secondary gates, twenty gates in all, distributed equally along the four sides of the square and strategically placed along each wall: the main gate in the middle of each wall and two secondary gates on each side. Therefore there were no gates but only openings where the roads ended. The walls did not need gates to support them. They were solid, thick from the base to a height of three metres, then narrowing progressively to the top, nine metres from the ground. Needless to say, the side entrances were served by roads forking from the main road at a convenient distance. And as one might expect, this simple geometrical layout was linked by means of suitable junctions to the general network of roads throughout the country. If everything ends up everywhere, everything would end up there.

The structure, four walls served by four roads, was a cemetery. And this cemetery was to be the only one in the land. This had been decided by the royal personage. When supreme greatness and supreme sensibility are united in a king, a single cemetery is possible. All kings are great, by definition and birth: any king who might wish otherwise will wish in vain (even the exceptions of other dynasties are great amongst their peers). But they may or may not be sensitive, and here one is not speaking of that common, plebeian sensibility, which expresses itself with a tear in the corner of an eye or by an irrepressible tremor on the lip, but of another sensibility, unprecedented to such a degree in the history of this nation and perhaps even of the universe: a sensibility incapable of confronting death or any of the paraphernalia and rituals associated with death, whether it be the mourning of relatives or the commercial manifestations of bereavement. Such was this king. Like all kings and presidents, he had to travel and visit his domains, to caress little children selected by protocol beforehand, to receive bouquets of flowers already inspected by the secret police in case they might have poison or a bomb concealed inside, to cut ribbons in fast, non-toxic colours. All this and more the King carried out with good grace. But each visit caused him endless suffering: death, nothing but death wherever one looked, signs of death everywhere, the pointed tip of a cypress tree, a widow's black shawl and, more than once, the unbearable sight of some funeral procession the master of ceremonies had inexcusably overlooked, or which, setting out late or early, unexpectedly appeared at the most solemn moment of all, just as the King was passing or about to pass. After these visits the King would return to his palace in a state of distress, convinced he was about to die. And the sorrows of others and his own fear of death caused him so much anguish that, one day when he was relaxing on the highest terrace in the palace and looking into the distance (this being the clearest day ever recorded not only throughout the history of that dynasty but throughout its entire civilization), he saw four resplendent white walls and these gave him the idea of building one central cemetery to be used by everyone.

For a nation accustomed for thousands of years to burying its dead in public for all to see, this provoked the most awful revolution. But those who feared revolution began to fear chaos, when the King's idea, with that resolute and rapid progress ideas make, especially when thought up by kings, went further and became what evil tongues described as delirium: all the cemeteries in the land had to be cleared of bones and remains, whatever their degree of decomposition, and put into new coffins which would be transported for burial in the new cemetery. Not even the royal ashes of the sovereign's ancestors were exempt from this mandate: a new pantheon would be built in a style probably inspired by the ancient Egyptian pyramids, and there, in due course, once calm was restored, their remains would be carried with all pomp and ceremony along the main northern road lined on either side with loyal subjects, until they eventually reached the final resting-place for the venerable bones of all those who had been crowned since the time when one man managed to persuade the others by means of words and force, saying: 'I want a crown on my head, make me one.' Some claim that this egalitarian decision helped more than anything to pacify those who saw themselves deprived of the remains of their dear departed. Another factor of some weight must have been the tacit satisfaction of all those who took the opposite view and were tired of the rules and traditions which turn the dead, because of the demands they make, into transitional beings between what is no longer life and a death that is not yet real. Suddenly everyone decided the King's idea was the best thing any man had ever conceived and no other nation could boast of having such a king, and since fate had decreed that the King should be born and reign there, it was up to the people to obey him gladly, also for the solace of the dead who were no less deserving. The history of nations knows moments of utter bliss: this was such a moment and this nation rejoiced.

When the cemetery was finally completed, the enormous task of disinterment began. At first it was easy: the thousands of existing cemeteries, large, medium and small, were also surrounded by walls, and, so to speak, within their perimeter it was enough to excavate to the stipulated depth of three feet for greater safety, and remove everything, cubic metre upon cubic metre of bones, rotten planks of wood, dismembered bodies shaken out of their coffins by the excavators; then the rubble had to be transferred into coffins of different sizes, for newborn babes as well as for the very old, emptying some bones or flesh into each of them at random, two skulls and four hands, odd bits of rib, a breast that was still firm along with a withered belly, a simple bone or hip, or one of Buddha's teeth, even the shoulder-blade of some saint or the blood missing from the miraculous phial of St Januarius. It was decided that each part of a corpse would count as a whole corpse, and they lined up the participants in this infinite funeral which came from every corner of the nation, carefully wending its way from villages, towns and cities, along routes which became increasingly wider as far as the main road network and from there, by means of junctions specially built, on to roads subsequently known as the roads of the dead.

In the beginning, as stated earlier, there were no problems. But then someone remembered, unless the idea came from the country's precious monarch, that before this ruling about cemeteries had been enforced, the dead had been buried everywhere, on mountains and in the valleys, in churchyards, under the shade of trees, beneath the floorboards of the very houses in which they had lived, in any convenient spot, and only a little deeper than the depth, for example, of a ploughshare. Not to mention the wars, the vast trenches for thousands of corpses, all over the world, from Asia and Europe and other continents, even though probably with fewer corpses, for naturally there had also been wars in this king's realm and therefore bodies had been buried at random. There was, it had to be confessed, a moment of great perplexity. The King himself, had this latest idea been his, would not have kept it to himself for that would have been impossible. New orders were given and, since the country could not be turned over from end to end, as the cemeteries had been turned over, wise men were summoned before the King to hear this injunction from his royal lips: with all possible haste they must invent instruments capable of detecting the presence of buried remains, just as instruments had been invented to find water or metal. It would be no mean feat, the wise men acknowledged, once gathered together. They spent three days in discussion and then each of them locked himself away in his own laboratory. The State coffers were opened once more, and a new general tax was imposed. The problem was finally resolved but, as always happens in such cases, not all at once. To give an example, the case of that wise man could be cited who invented an instrument which lit up and made a noise whenever it encountered a body, but it had one serious drawback insofar as it could not distinguish between live or dead bodies. As a result, this instrument, handled of course by living people, behaved like someone possessed, screeching and flashing its indicators in a frenzy, torn between all the reactions from both the living and the dead surrounding it, and in the end, incapable of providing any reliable information. The entire nation mocked this unfortunate scientist, then lavished tributes and honours on him several months later, when he found the solution by introducing into the instrument a kind of memory or fixed idea. If one listened attentively, it was possible to detect a constant sound coming from inside the mechanism which went on repeating: 'I must only find dead bodies or remains, I must only find dead bodies or remains, dead bodies or remains, or remains . . .'

Fortunately, there was one remaining drawback, as we shall see. No sooner did the instrument begin to function than people realised that, this time, it could not tell the difference between human and non-human bodies, but this new flaw, which explains why I earlier used the word fortunately, turned out to be an advantage: when the King understood the danger he had escaped, he had the shivers: in fact, all death is death, even the non-human kind, and there would be no purpose in removing dead men from sight, when dogs, horses and birds go on dropping before our eyes. And all other creatures, with the possible exception of insects which are only half-animal (as was firmly believed by the nation's scientists at that time). Then a full-scale investigation was ordered, a Cyclopean task which went on for years. Not so much as a hand-breadth of land remained to be examined, even in places which had been uninhabited for as long as anyone could remember: not even the highest mountains escaped or the deepest rivers, where thousands of dead bodies were discovered; the deepest roots did not escape, sometimes entangled around the remains of someone higher up who had been trying, out of desire or necessity, to reach the sap of some tree. Nor did the roads escape, which had to be lifted in many places and rebuilt. Finally, the kingdom found itself released from death. One day, when the King himself formally announced that the country was cleansed of death (his words), he declared a public holiday and national rejoicing. On such days it is customary for more people than usual to die, because of accidents, muggings, etc., but the National Life Service (as it was called) employed rapid, up-to-date methods: once death had been confirmed, the corpse followed the shortest route to the great highway of corpses, which had inevitably come to be known as no-man's-land. Having got rid of the dead, the King could be happy. As for the people, they would have to get used to it.

The first thing to be restored was a sense of tranquillity, that calm of natural mortality which allows families to be spared bereavement for years on end, and sometimes for many years if these families are not numerous. It could be said without exaggeration that the removal period was a time of national mourning in the strictest sense of that expression, a mourning which came from the depths of the earth. To smile during those years of sorrow would have been, for anyone who dared, an act of moral degradation: it is unseemly to smile when a relative, however distant, is being carried to the grave, intact or in pieces, and is tipped out from the bucket of an excavator on high into a new coffin, so much for each coffin, like filling moulds for sweets or bricks. After that lengthy period when people went around with an expression of noble and serene sorrow, smiles returned, then laughter, even guffaws and outbursts of derision and mockery, preceded by irony and humour; all of this regained some sign of life or renewed its hidden struggle against death.

But this tranquillity was not merely that of a soul back on the same old rails after a grand collision, but also that of the body, because words cannot express what all that effort sustained over such a long period of time meant for those who were still alive. It was not only the public works, the opening up of roads, the building of bridges, tunnels, viaducts, it was not only the scientific research, of which a pale and fragmentary idea has already been given; it was also the industry in timber, from the felling of trees (forest upon forest) to the sawing of planks, the drying out by means of accelerated processes, to the fittings for urns and coffins which required the installation of huge mechanical assembly lines for mass production; it also meant, as previously stated, the temporary reconversion of the metal industry in order to meet the demand for machinery and other material, starting with nails and hinges; then textiles and braidings for linings and decorations; then the quarrying for marble and stonework which, in its turn, suddenly began disembowelling the earth in order to supply so many tombstones and headstones ornately carved or plain; and those minority occupations almost akin to crafts, such as painting letters in black and gold, touching up photographs, panel-beating and glazing, that of artificial flowers, the making of candles and tapers, etc., etc., etc. But perhaps the greatest contribution of all, without which none of the work could have gone ahead, was that of the transport industry. No words could express the amount of effort put into the manufacturing of trucks and other heavy vehicles, an industry obliged in its turn to reconvert itself, to modify its production plans, to organise new sequences of assembly before delivering the coffins to the new cemetery: try to imagine the complications involved in planning integrated time-tables, the periods of disruption and convergence, the continuous flow of incoming traffic with ever increasing loads, and all this having to harmonise with the normal circulation of the living, whether on working days or public holidays, whether travelling to work or for pleasure, without forgetting the infra-structure: restaurants and inns all along the route so that lorry-drivers might be able to eat and sleep, car parks for the larger vehicles, some distractions to relieve the pressures of mind and body, telephone lines, the installations for emergencies and first-aid, workshops for electrical and mechanical repairs, garages for petrol, oil, diesel, tyres, spare parts, etc. And this in turn clearly boosted other industries in a cycle of mutual regeneration, producing wealth to the extent of maximum output and full employment. As was only to be expected, this revival was followed by a depression, and no one was surprised because it had been foreseen by the economic pundits. The negative effect of this depression was generously compensated, as the social psychologists had forecast, because of the irrepressible desire for respite which began to manifest itself among the people once their output had reached the point of saturation. They were embarking on a new phase of normality.

In the geometrical centre of the country, open to the four winds, stands the cemetery. Much less than a quarter of its hundred square kilometres was occupied by transferred corpses, and this prompted a group of mathematicians to try and demonstrate, with the figures to hand, that the land needed for these reburials would have to be much bigger, taking into consideration the likely number of deaths since the country was first populated and the average amount of space needed for each corpse, even discounting those who, reduced to dust and ashes, were beyond recovery. The enigma, if it could be called that, was to exercise the minds of future generations, like the squaring of the circle or the duplication of the cube, because the wise devotees of disciplines related to biology proved in the presence of the King that not a single corpse worthy of the name remained to be disinterred throughout the entire country. After some deep reflection, the King, torn between trust and scepticism, passed a decree which declared the matter closed; the decisive argument for him was the sense of relief he experienced when he returned from his travels and visits; if he no longer saw death it was because death had finally withdrawn.

The occupation of the cemetery, although the initial plan conformed to more rational criteria, went from the periphery to the centre. First near the gates and up against the walls, then following a curve which began almost perfectly radial and gradually became cycloid, this, too, being a transitional phase whose future plays no part in our story. But this internal moulding, as it were, undulating along the walls and isolated by them, was reflected almost symmetrically, even during the removal, in a form that matched faithfully on the outside. No one had suspected that this might happen, but there were those who asserted that only a fool could have failed to foresee the outcome.

The first sign, like the tiniest of spores about to sprout into a plant, then into a tuft, then into a thick cluster, and finally impenetrable scrub, was an improvised stall for the sale of soft drinks and spirits beside one of the secondary gates on the south wall. Even though revived for the journey, the transport workers felt they would find even greater refreshment there. Then other tiny shops sprang up nearby at the other gates, and began selling identical or similar goods, and those who ran them soon felt the need to set up house there, primitive huts on stilts to begin with, then using more durable materials, such as bricks, stones and tiles. It is worth observing in passing that from the moment these first buildings appeared, one could distinguish a) almost imperceptibly, b) from the evidence before one's eyes, the social status, as it were, of the four sides of the square. As with all countries, this one, too, was not uniformly populated, nor, despite His Majesty's extraordinary complacency, were his subjects socially equal: some were rich and others poor, and the distribution of the former and the latter conformed to universal criteria: the poor man attracts the rich man at a distance that suits the rich man; in his turn, the rich man attracts the poor man, but that is not to say that the outcome (the constant factor in the process) will operate in the poor man's favour. If, because of the criteria applied to the living, the cemetery, after this general transfer, began to divide up internally, it also became noticeable on the outside. There is scarcely any need to explain why. Since the northern region had the highest concentration of the country's wealthy people, that side of the cemetery, with its imposing outlay, assumed a social status opposed, for example, to that of the south, which happened to service the poorest region. And the same thing occurred, in general, when it came to the other sides. Like attracts like. Although in a much less clearly defined manner, the outside reflected the inside. For example, the florists who soon began appearing on all four sides of the square did not all sell the same quality of goods: some displayed and sold the most exquisite blooms cultivated in gardens and hothouses at great expense, others were more modest and sold flowers gathered from the surrounding countryside. The same could be said about all the other goods displayed there, and as one might have expected, the civil servants complained, on finding themselves weighed down with petitions and complaints. One must not forget that the cemetery had a complicated system of administration, controlled its own budget, employed thousands of grave-diggers. In the early days, the different categories of civil servants lived inside the square, in the central part, and well out of sight of any burials. But soon there were problems regarding hierarchy, provisions, schools for the children, hospitals, maternity care. What was to be done? Build a city within the cemetery? That would mean going back to the beginning, not to mention that with the passage of time the city and the cemetery would overlap, the tombs penetrating gaps in the streets or actually bordering the pavements, the streets circling the tombs in search of land for the houses. It would mean returning to the same old promiscuity, now aggravated by the fact that things happened within a square of ten kilometres on each side with few exits to the outside. So now it was a question of choosing between a city of living human beings surrounded by a city of the dead, or the only alternative, a city of the dead surrounded by four cities of living human beings. Once the choice was formalised, and it also became clear that those accompanying the funeral processions could not make the long, exhausting return journey immediately, either because they did not have the strength or because incapable of sudden separation from their loved ones, the four external cities grew apace in haphazard fashion. There were boarding-houses of every category in every street, hotels with one, two, three, four, five stars or more, numerous brothels, churches for every legally recognised cult and several secret sects, little corner shops and enormous department stores, countless houses, office buildings, public offices and various municipal bodies. Then came public transport, the police, restricted circulation and the problem of traffic. And a certain amount of delinquency. One fiction alone was preserved: to keep the dead out of sight of the living; therefore no building could be more than nine metres high. But this matter was solved later, when an imaginative architect reinvented Columbus's egg: walls higher than nine metres for buildings higher than nine metres.

In the fullness of time the cemetery wall became unrecognisable: instead of the initial smooth uniformity extended for forty kilometres, what appeared was an irregular denticulation, also variable in width and height, according to the side of the wall. No one can any longer remember when it was decided that the time had come to install the cemetery gates. The civil servant who had pressed for this economy had already passed on to the other side and could no longer defend a theory that was sound at the time but no longer tenable, as he himself would have had the good sense to acknowledge: stories began circulating about souls from the other world, about ghosts and apparitions – so what else could be done but to install gates?

And so four great cities rose up between the kingdom and the cemetery, each one facing its cardinal point, four unexpected cities which came to be known as Northern Cemetery, Southern Cemetery, Eastern Cemetery and Western Cemetery, but which were later simply referred to as Cemeteries Number One, Two, Three and Four, inasmuch as all attempts to give them more poetic or commemorative names had failed. These four cities acted as four barriers, four living walls which surrounded and protected the cemetery. The cemetery represented one hundred square kilometres of almost total silence and solitude, surrounded by the outer anthill of the living, by the sound of people shouting, hooters, outbursts of laughter and snatches of conversation, the rumbling of engines, by the interminable murmuring of nerve-cells. To arrive at the cemetery was already something of an adventure. Eventually nobody could retrace the rectilinear plan of the old roads within the cities. It was easy to say where they had passed: you only had to stand in front of one of the main gates. But leaving aside some of the longer stretches of recognisable paving, the rest had got lost in the confusion of buildings and roads, improvised to begin with and then superimposed on the original plan. Only in the open countryside was the road still the highway of the dead.

And now the inevitable happened, although we do not know who started it or when. A summary investigation, carried out afterwards, verified cases on the outer periphery of City Number Two, the poorest city of all, and facing south, as we stated earlier: corpses buried in small private backyards beneath flowering plants which reappeared each spring. About this same time, like those great inventions which erupt in various minds simultaneously because the time has come for them to mature, in sparsely populated parts of the realm certain persons decided, for many different and sometimes contradictory reasons, to bury their dead near, or inside caves, at the side of forest paths or on some sheltered mountain slope. There were fewer prosecutions in those days and many civil servants were prepared to accept bribes. The statistics bureau announced that, according to the official registers, a lower mortality rate could be safely predicted, and this was naturally attributed to the government's health programme, under the direct supervision of His Majesty the King. The four cities of the cemetery felt the consequences of the decline in the number of deaths. Certain businesses suffered serious losses, there were a fair number of bankruptcies, some of them fraudulent, and when it was finally recognised that, however laudable, the royal strategy for the nation's welfare was not likely to concede immortality, a thoroughly repressive law was introduced to enforce the obedience of the masses. To no avail: after a short-lived outburst of enthusiasm, the cities stagnated and became dilapidated. Ever so slowly, the kingdom began to be repopulated with the dead. In the end, the vast central cemetery only received corpses from the four surrounding cities, which became increasingly deserted and silent. But the King was no longer there to see it.

The King was now very old. One day, looking down from the highest terrace of the palace, he saw, despite failing eyesight, the pointed tip of a cypress tree rising above four white walls, in all probability indicating the presence of a courtyard rather than death. But one divines certain things without difficulty, especially as one gets older. The King stored every item of news and every rumour in his head, what they told him and what they kept from him, and he realised the hour of understanding had come. Followed by a guard, as protocol demanded, he descended into the palace gardens. Dragging his royal cloak, he slowly made his way along an avenue leading to the concealed heart of the forest. There he lay down in a clearing and stretched out on the dry leaves; then summoning the guard who had fallen to his knees, he told him before dying: 'Here'.

Things

As it closed, the tall, heavy door caught the back of the civil servant's right hand and left a deep scratch, red but scarcely bleeding. The skin had been torn here and there, raised in several spots which began to hurt, for the uneven surface and roughness of the wood had not exerted the continuous pressure or prolonged contact likely to cause an open wound or pull back the skin thereby allowing the blood to gush out and quickly spread. Before going to the tiny office where he was due to sign on in ten minutes and work a five-hour stretch, the civil servant made his way to the First Aid Room (FAR) to have the wound dressed: his work brought him into contact with the public and there was something unsightly about that scratch. As he was disinfecting the wound, the nurse, on being told how the accident had happened, commented that this was the third such case that day. Caused by the same door.

—I suppose they'll take it off, he added.

Using a brush, he smeared over the scratch a colourless liquid which quickly dried, taking on the colour of his skin.

And not just the colour but also the opaque texture of skin, so that no one would have suspected anything had happened. Only by looking very closely would anyone be able to see that the scratch had been covered. At a quick glance there was nothing to be seen.

—Tomorrow you can pull off the film. Twelve hours should be sufficient.

The nurse looked worried. He asked him:

—Have you heard about the settee? The large one that was in the waiting-room.

—No. I've just arrived for the afternoon shift.

—It had to be removed. It's in the other room.

—Why?

—We don't exactly know. The doctor examined it immediately, but made no diagnosis. Not that it was necessary. A member of the public complained that the settee was getting overheated. And he was right. I checked it myself.

—No doubt the manufacturer's fault.

—Yes. Probably. The temperature is too high. On any other occasion, and the doctor agreed, it would have been treated as a case of fever.

—Well, it's not unknown. Two years ago there was a similar case. A friend of mine had to return an overcoat as good as new to the factory. He found it impossible to wear.

—And then what?

—Nothing. The factory exchanged it. And he had no further cause for complaint.

He looked at his watch: he still had ten minutes. Or was he mistaken? He could have sworn that when he injured his hand he had exactly ten minutes left. Or had he forgotten today to consult his watch on entering the building?

—Can I take a look at the settee?

The nurse opened a glass door.

—It's in there.

The settee was long enough to seat four people and although it had obviously been used it was still in good condition.

—Would you like to try it? asked the nurse.

The civil servant sat down.

—Well?

—It's rather uncomfortable. Is the treatment having any effect?

—I'm giving it injections every hour. So far, I haven't noticed any difference. It's time for another injection.

He prepared the syringe, sucked in the contents of a large ampoule and briskly stuck the needle into the settee.

—And if there's no improvement? the civil servant enquired.

—The doctor will decide. This is the treatment he prescribed. If it doesn't work, there's nothing more to be done and the settee goes back to the factory.

—Fine. I'm off to work. Thanks.

In the corridor he checked the time again. Still ten minutes to go. Could his watch have stopped? He put it to his ear: the tick-tock could be clearly heard, although somewhat muffled, but the hands were not moving. He realised he was going to be very late in arriving. He hated being late. The public would not suffer, since the colleague from whom he was taking over was not allowed to leave the office until he arrived. Before pushing open the door, he took another look at his watch: the same as before. On hearing him come in, his colleague got to his feet, said a few words to the people waiting on the other side of the counter window, then closed it. That was the rule. Civil servants took over from each other without delay but the counter window always had to be closed.

—You're late.

—I'm afraid so. Sorry.

—It's a quarter past the hour. I ought to report you.

—Of course. My watch stopped. That's why I'm late. But, strangely enough, it's still going.

—It's still going?

—Don't you believe me? Take a look.

They both looked at the watch.

—That's very odd.

—Look at the hands. They're not moving. But you can hear the tick-tock.

—Yes, so you can. I'll say nothing about your lateness this time, considering, but I think you should tell the supervisor what is happening to your watch.

—I suppose so.

—There have been lots of curious things happening in recent weeks.

—The Government is on its guard and is almost certain to take measures.

Someone knocked on the shiny plate glass of the window. The two civil servants signed the time-sheet.

—Be careful with the main door, warned the one who was starting the shift.

—Did you get a nasty bump? Then you're the third person today.

—And did you hear about the settee having a fever?

—Everybody knows.

—Isn't it strange?

—It is, although it's not uncommon. See you on Monday.

—Have a nice weekend.

He opened the window. There were three people waiting. He apologised, as the rule book instructed, and took from the first man – tall, smartly dressed and middle-aged – an identity card. He slotted it into the machine, checked the luminous symbols which came up on the screen before returning the card:

—Now then. What can I do for you? Please be brief. These, too, were the phrases stipulated by the rule book. The man replied without a moment's hesitation:

—I'll be brief. I want a piano.

—We don't get many requests for pianos nowadays. Tell me. Do you really need one?

—Are they so difficult to obtain?

—The raw materials are scarce. When do you need it?

—Within fifteen days.

—You might as well ask for the moon. A piano requires raw materials of the highest quality, and they're in short supply, if that makes my meaning any clearer.

—This piano is for a birthday present. Do you understand?

—Perfectly. But you should have placed your order sooner.

—It wasn't possible. Let me remind you, I'm registered in one of the highest categories.

As he spoke these words, the client opened his right hand with the palm turned upwards to display a green C tattooed on the palm. The civil servant looked at the letter, then at the luminous symbols on the screen and nodded his head in affirmation:

—I've taken special note. You'll have your piano within fifteen days.

—Many thanks. Do you want me to pay in full or will a deposit be enough?

—A deposit is fine.

The man took a wallet from his pocket and put the required amount of money on the counter. The notes were rectangular and made of fine, soft paper in one colour but in different shades, just as the tiny emblematic portraits which determined their value were also different. The civil servant counted them. As he gathered them together and was about to put them away into the safe, one of the notes suddenly curled up and wrapped itself tightly round one finger. The client said:

—The same thing happened to me today. The Mint ought to be more careful when printing notes.

—Have you lodged a formal complaint?

—Naturally, I considered it my duty.

—Very well. The Inspection Department can investigate both complaints, yours and mine. Here are the documents. On the date written there present yourself at the delivery office. But since you're in category C, I assume the piano will be despatched to your home.

—That is what normally happens when I order something. Good afternoon.

—Good afternoon.

Five hours later the civil servant found himself once more at the main door. He reached out for the handle, carefully calculated the distance and, with one quick movement, opened the door and passed safely to the other side. With a muffled noise that sounded like a sigh, the automatic door slowly began to close. It was almost night. Working the second shift had its advantages: a better class of people, quality products, and no need to get up early in the morning, although in the winter when the days are shorter it could be a little depressing to go from the brightly lit office into the twilight, much too early and also much too late. Yet, although the sky was unusually overcast, this was late summer and the short stroll was altogether pleasant.

He did not live far away. There was not even enough time to see the city transform itself as dusk began to fall. In rain or sunshine, he covered the few hundred metres on foot because taxi-drivers were not allowed to pick up passengers for such short journeys and no buses passed along his street. Slipping his hands into his coat pockets, he could feel the letter he had forgotten to drop into the pillar-box when he set out for the Department of Special Requisitions (DSR) where he worked. He kept the letter in his hand in order not to forget a second time and used the underpass to get onto the other side of the avenue. Walking behind him were two women chatting to each other:

—You can't imagine the state my husband was in this morning. Not to mention myself, but he was the first to notice what had happened.

—Honestly, it's enough to drive anybody mad.

—We both stood there in amazement, looking at each other.

—But surely you must have heard something during the night?

—Not a thing. Neither of us.

The voices died away. The women had turned into an underpass going off in another direction. The civil servant mumbled to himself 'What on earth were they talking about?' And this made him think about the day's events, about his right hand clutching the letter inside his pocket, the deep scratch the door had inflicted, about the settee suffering from fever, his watch which went on ticking with the hands still indicating there were ten minutes to go before he was due to start work. And the note tightly wrapped round one finger. There had always been such incidents, nothing too serious, simply inconvenient, but too frequent for his liking. Despite the efforts of the Government (G), it had proved impossible to avoid them, and no one seriously expected otherwise. There was a time when the manufacturing process had reached such a degree of perfection and faults became so rare that the Government (G) decided there was little point in depriving members of the public (especially those in categories A, B and C) of their civil right and pleasure to lodge complaints: a wise decision which could only benefit the manufacturing industry. So factories were instructed to lower their standards. This decision, however, could not be blamed for the poor quality of the goods which had been flooding the market for the last two months. As someone employed in the Department of Special Requisitions (DSR), he was in a good position to know that the Government had revoked these instructions more than a month ago and imposed new standards to ensure maximum quality. Without achieving any results. As far as he could remember, this incident with the door was certainly the most disturbing. It was not a case of some object or other, or some simple utensil, or even a piece of furniture, such as the settee in the entrance-hall, but of an item of imposing dimensions; although the settee was anything but small. However, it formed part of the interior furnishings, while the door was an integral part of the building, if not the most important part. After all, it is the door that transforms a space which is simply circumscribed into a closed space. In the end, the Government (G) appointed a committee to examine the situation and make some proposals. The best computer equipment available had been put at the disposal of this group of experts, which included not only specialists in electronics but leading scholars in the fields of sociology, psychology and anatomy, whose collaboration was crucial in such matters. The committee had been given fifteen days in which to present its report and recommendations. They still had ten days left but the situation was obviously getting worse.

The rain began falling, a drizzle of watery dust, light and airy. In the distance, the civil servant could see the pillar-box where he must deposit the letter. He thought: 'I mustn't forget this time.' A huge covered lorry turned the nearby corner and went past him. It carried an advertisement in bold letters: 'Carpets and rugs'. There went a dream he had never succeeded in fulfilling: to carpet his apartment. But one day, if everything went according to plan. The lorry went past. The pillar-box had disappeared. The civil servant surmised he had lost his bearings, that he had changed direction when he started thinking about carpets after seeing the advertisement. He looked around him bewildered, but also surprised to find that he was not afraid. Nothing except a vague sense of uneasiness, perhaps nervousness, like someone grappling with a problem he cannot quite solve. There was no sign of a pillar-box. He approached the spot where it should be standing, where it had stood for so many years, with its cylindrical body painted blue and that rectangular orifice, a mouth forever gaping and silent and giving access to its belly. The soil where the pillar-box had once stood was still dry and showed signs of having been recently disturbed. A policeman came running up to him:

—Did you see it disappear? he enquired.

—No. But I almost did. Had it not been for a lorry passing in front of me, I'd have seen it.

The policeman was taking down notes. Then he closed his notebook and, with his foot, pushed aside a clod of earth which had been brought up from the cavity on to street level and said in the tone of voice of someone who is simply thinking aloud:

—Had you been watching, the pillar-box would probably still be here.

And he walked off, at the same time fondling the holster of his revolver.

The civil servant from the Department of Special Requisitions (DSR) went round the entire district before finding another pillar-box. This one had not disappeared. He quickly put his letter inside and, once he heard it fall into the net at the bottom, he retraced his steps. He thought: 'And suppose this pillar-box were also to disappear? What will happen to my letter?' It was not the letter (which was of no great importance) that was worrying him, but the situation which could almost be described as metaphysical. At the tobacconist's he bought an evening newspaper which he folded and stuffed into his pocket. The rain was getting heavier. At the spot where the pillar-box had disappeared, a tiny puddle had already formed. A woman sheltering under an umbrella arrived with a letter. Only at the last minute did she realise there was something amiss.

—Where's the pillar-box? she asked.

—It isn't here, replied the civil servant.

The woman was furious:

—They can't do this. Removing the pillar-box without warning the residents. We should all protest.

And she turned away, declaring aloud that next day she would be lodging a formal complaint.

The apartment block where the civil servant lived was nearby. He opened the door with the utmost caution while inwardly scolding himself: 'Scared of a door. Whatever next?' He switched on the stair-light and made his way to the lift. Hanging from the grating was a notice: 'Out of Order'. He was annoyed, irritated, not so much because he had to climb the stairs (he only lived on the second floor) but because on the fifth landing of the stairway three steps had been missing for the past week which meant residents had to take certain precautions and tread carefully. The Department of General Maintenance (DGM) was not doing its job properly. At any other time, the Administration would have been accused of incompetence, of having too much work on their hands, of not employing enough staff or failing to supply the raw materials. On this occasion, however, there had to be some other explanation and he preferred not to think about it. He climbed the stairs, taking his time, preparing himself mentally for the little acrobatic feat he would have to perform: to hop over the void created by those three missing steps by leaping upwards, making it all the more difficult, and extending his legs with all his might. Then he noticed that there were not three steps missing but four. He rebuked himself once more, this time for being so forgetful, and after several unsuccessful attempts he managed to reach the step above.

Being unmarried, he lived alone. He prepared his own meals, sent his clothes to the laundry and enjoyed his work. Generally speaking, he considered himself a contented man. How could he be otherwise: the country was being managed admirably, duties were equitably shared out, the Government was competent and had proved its ability to galvanise industry. As for these more recent problems, they too would be resolved in time. Since it was still too early to eat, he sat down to read the newspaper as usual, unconsciously inventing the same futile justification, or rather, unaware of its futility. On the first page there was a Formal Statement (FS) from the Government about the faults discovered of late in various objects, utensils, machines and installations. Reassurances were given that the situation was not serious and would soon be remedied once the committee appointed to investigate these matters and which now had a specialist in parapsychology among its members got to work. No mention was made of things suddenly disappearing.

Neatly folding the newspaper, he put it on a low table at his feet. He glanced at the time on the wall clock: a few minutes to go before the television programme started. His daily routine had been disrupted by events, especially by the disappearance of the pillar-box which had made him lose precious time. Normally he had time to read the newspaper from beginning to end, to prepare himself a simple dinner, settle down in front of the screen and listen to the news while he ate. Then he would take his plate, glass and cutlery into the kitchen, and return to his armchair where he would sit watching the programme or doze off until it ended. He asked himself how he would manage today without trying to find an answer. Reaching out, he switched on the set: he heard a hissing sound, the screen gradually lit up until the test card appeared, a complicated system of vertical, horizontal and diagonal lines, with light and dark surfaces. He stopped looking, absent-mindedly, as if hypnotised by that motionless image. He lit a cigarette (he never smoked on duty, for it was forbidden) and sat down again. He remembered to look at his wrist watch: still not working and he could no longer hear the tick-tock. He undid the black strap, put the watch down on the table alongside the newspaper and gave a deep sigh. A loud click made him turn round in a flash. 'Some piece of furniture', he thought to himself. And at that very moment the test card vanished and suddenly there appeared a child's face with eyes wide open. It receded into the background, far back into the remote distance until it became a simple luminous dot, quivering in the centre of the black screen. Next minute the test card reappeared, slightly tremulous, undulating, like an image reflected in water. Puzzled, the civil servant stroked his face. He picked up the telephone and called the Television Information Service (TIS) and when they answered, he enquired:

—Can you tell me what is causing the interference on my test card?

A male voice curtly replied:

—There is no interference.

—I'm sorry, but I have just seen it with my own eyes.

—We have no information to give you.

His call was cut off. 'I must have done something wrong. There has to be some connection,' he murmured. He went and sat in front of the screen, where the test card had resumed its hypnotic inertia. A succession of clicks could be heard, getting louder and louder. He could not locate them. They seemed so close, yet so remote, under his feet or somewhere in the building. He got up again and opened the window: the rain had stopped. Anyway, this was not the rainy season. Something must have broken down in the Meteorological Unit (MU): during the summer months it never rained. From the window he could see quite clearly where the pillar-box had been set in the ground. He took a deep breath, filling his lungs, looked up at the sky which was now clear and speckled with stars, the brightest of them outshining the neon lights in the city centre. The television programme was just starting. He returned to his chair. He wanted to hear the news bulletin at the start of the programme. A woman with a tense, artificial smile announced the evening's programme, and then came the arpeggios as a prelude to the news. A male announcer with an emaciated face read out a Formal Statement (FS) released by the Government. He announced: 'The Government wishes to inform members of the public that the faults and defects in certain objects, utensils, machines and installations (OUMIs, in abbreviated form), which have become increasingly common in recent months, are being scrupulously examined by a panel of experts which now includes a parapsychologist. Members of the public should beware of anyone spreading rumours or trying to provoke panic and hysteria. Citizens should remain calm even when the aforesaid OUMIs start disappearing: objects, utensils, machines or installations. Everyone should be on their guard. Every OUMI (object, utensil, machine or installation) should be carefully examined in future. The Government wishes to stress the importance of sighting any OUMI (object, utensil, machine or installation), the moment it starts to disappear. Anyone who can give detailed information or prevent the disappearance of OUMIs will be duly rewarded and promoted to category C if classified in a lower category. The Government is counting on public support and trust.' There were other items of news but less interesting. The rest of the programme was just as dull, apart from a documentary about manufacturing carpets. Disgruntled, as if he had been personally insulted, he switched off the receiver: classified in category H (he opened his right hand and saw the green letter), he would have to save for ages before he could afford the carpet he had dreamed about all these years. He knew perfectly well how carpets were manufactured. He found it downright offensive that such documentaries should be shown to people who had nothing to cover their floors.

Moving into the kitchen, he prepared dinner. He scrambled some eggs which he ate with a slice of bread and drank a glass of wine, perched at a corner of the kitchen table. Then he washed up the few dishes he had used. He kept his injured hand out of the water even though he knew that this biological film was waterproof: it acted as another skin regenerating the organic tissues and, like skin, it breathed. Anyone with serious burns would not die if covered at once with this biological liquid and only the pain would prevent the victim from leading a normal life until completely cured. He put away his plate and the frying-pan, and just as he was about to deposit his glass beside the only other two glasses he possessed, he saw an empty space in the cupboard. At first he could not recall what had been there before. Holding the glass in one hand, he stood there gaping, searching in his memory, trying hard to remember. That was it: the large jug he rarely used. He slowly placed the glass alongside the others and closed the cupboard door. Then he remembered the advice given by the Government (G) and re-opened it. Everything was in its place, except the jug. He searched the entire kitchen, moving each object with the greatest care, examining them carefully one by one, before acknowledging three facts: the jug was not where he had left it, not in the kitchen, nowhere in the house. Therefore it must have disappeared.

He did not panic. After hearing the Formal Statement (FS) on the Television (TV), he felt proud to be a civil servant, a loyal citizen serving in a huge army of vigilantes. He saw himself in direct communication with the Government (G), someone in authority perhaps destined to become a distinguished figure in the city and country one day, and deserving of category C.

He returned to the sitting-room with a proud, martial stride: went to the window which he had left open. With a commanding glance he looked up and down the street and decided he would spend his weekend carrying out surveillance throughout the city. It would be a stroke of bad luck if he should fail to get some useful information for the Government (G), useful enough to warrant his promotion to category C. He had never been ambitious but the moment had now arrived to claim his legitimate rights. Category C would at least give him much greater responsibility in the Department of Special Requisitions (DSR), it might even mean being transferred to a department closer to Central Government (CG). He opened his hand, saw the letter H, imagined a C in its place, relished the vision of the new skin they would graft on to the palm of his hand. He moved away from the window and switched on the television: the lamination stage in the process of manufacturing carpets was being demonstrated. His interest aroused, he settled down comfortably in his chair and watched the programme to the end. The same male announcer read the latest news bulletin, repeated the Government's Formal Statement (FM), then went on to declare, without clarifying any eventual connection between the two items of news, that next day the entire periphery of the city would be under the surveillance of three squadrons of helicopters, and that the Supreme Command of the Air Force (SCAF) had given every reassurance that this surveillance would be backed up with other military equipment if necessary. The civil servant switched off the television and went to bed. There was no more rain during the night but the whole building never stopped creaking. Woken from their sleep, some tenants took fright and telephoned the police and fire-brigade. They were assured the situation was under control, that human lives would be protected, but no such guarantee could be given, alas, regarding the safety of property, although precautions were being taken. And people must read the Government's Formal Statement (FS). The civil servant from the DSR slept soundly.

When he left his apartment the next morning, he met some neighbours conversing on the landing. The lift was working again. Just as well, they all agreed, for there were now twenty steps missing between the second and ground floor. On the floors above, many more steps were missing. The neighbours were concerned and questioned the civil servant from the DSR. In his opinion the situation would get worse before it got better, but he assured them things would soon be back to normal. This would be followed by a phase of recovery.

—Everyone knows there have been moments of crisis in the past. Manufacturing blunders, bad planning, not enough pressure, inferior raw materials. And everything has always sorted itself out.

A neighbour reminded him:

—But there's never been a crisis as serious as this one or that has lasted so long. Where shall we go if the OUMIs go on disappearing like this?

And her husband (category E):

—If the Government can't cope, then let's elect one that will show some initiative.

The civil servant agreed and got into the lift. But before he could press the button, his neighbour warned him:

—You won't find any door to the building downstairs. It disappeared during the night.

When the civil servant walked out of the lift into the hallway, he was shocked to find a square gap opening up before him. There was no other trace of the door except for the holes on the smooth surface where the hinges had been embedded. No evidence of any vandalism, no sign of any fragments. People were walking along the street but did not stop. The civil servant found their indifference almost insulting, but all became clear when he stepped onto the pavement: not only was the main door to his building missing, but all the other doors on both sides of the street. And not just the doors. Some shops no longer had any front or windows displaying goods. In one building the entire front wall had gone, as if it had been cut out from top to bottom with a very sharp knife. Anyone passing could peer right inside and see all the furnishings and people moving about at the back in a state of terror. For some strange reason all the ceiling lamps were lit: the building looked like an illuminated tree. On the first floor a woman could be heard shouting: 'My clothes? Where are my clothes?' And stark naked she crossed the room in full view of the street. The civil servant could not suppress a smile of amusement because the woman was enormous and shapeless. By Monday, there would be severe pressure on Normal Supplies (NS). The situation was becoming increasingly complicated. Just as well he worked in the DSR. He walked down the street, keeping a watchful eye on everything, inanimate or mobile, looking out for any suspicious behaviour as the Government (G) requested. He noticed others doing exactly the same and he found this demonstration of civic awareness reassuring although each and every one of them, in a manner of speaking, was competing for category C. 'There will be room for everyone,' he thought to himself.

There were certainly lots of people on the street. It was a bright, sunny morning, an ideal day for the beach or an outing into the countryside, or for staying at home and enjoying a restful weekend, were it not for the fact that homes no longer guaranteed safety, not in the literal sense of the word, but in that other sense which we must never forget: privacy. That nearby block stripped of its façade was not a pleasant sight: all those apartments exposed to passers-by and that fat woman going back and forth, probably unaware, without a stitch of clothing on her body, and whom could he question about her? He broke into a cold sweat at the thought of how embarrassed he would feel if the façade of his building were also to disappear and he were to find himself exposed (even fully clothed) to the public, without that dense, opaque shield which protected him from heat and cold, and from the curiosity of his fellow citizens. 'Perhaps', he thought to himself, 'this is the result of building with inferior materials. In that case one has to be grateful. Circumstances will rid the city of this abuse and the Government (G) will ascertain beyond a shadow of doubt what has to be put right and what avoided in future. Any delay would be criminal. The city and its inhabitants must be protected.' He went into a tobacconist's to buy a newspaper. The owner was having a chat over the counter with two customers:

— . . . and all of them were killed. The Radio still hasn't broadcast the news, but I heard it from a reliable source. A customer who was in here half-an-hour ago, at most, lives right beside the building and he saw what happened with his own eyes.

The civil servant from the DSR asked:

—What are you talking about?

And he opened his hand with a gesture meant to appear natural but calculated to put pressure on his audience: no one there appeared to be in a category higher than H. The tobacconist repeated his story:

—I was telling you what a customer told me. In the street where he lives, a whole block of flats has disappeared and all the residents were found lying dead on the ground, naked. Not so much as a ring on their fingers. The strangest thing of all is that the building should have vanished completely. Only a hole in the ground was left.

The news was serious. Faults in doors, the disappearance of pillar-boxes and jugs were bearable. One could even accept the façade of a building vanishing into thin air. But not that people should be killed. In a grave voice (the three men, with gestures also intended to convey a certain nonchalance or distraction, had turned up the palms of their hands: the owner of the shop was in category L, one of the customers was fortunate enough to be in category I, while the other one tried not to flaunt his N) the civil servant confided his civic indignation:

—From now on we're at war. War without quarter. I feel certain the Government will not tolerate any such provocation, let alone deaths. There will be reprisals.

The customer in category I, who was only one grade below his own, was bold enough to express some doubt:

—Unfortunately we're the ones who will suffer the consequences of any reprisals.

—Yes, I agree. But only in the short term. Don't forget, only in the short term.

The tobacconist:

—In fact, it's always been the same.

The civil servant picked up a newspaper and paid. On making this gesture, he remembered that he had not removed the biological film the male nurse had brushed on to his right hand. Never mind, he could remove it at any time. He said goodbye, departed and walked along the street until he reached the main avenue. As people passed him, they were chatting with excitement and gathering in small groups. Some looked worried, others as if they had slept badly or not at all. He joined a large group being addressed by an official of the Armed Forces (AF).

—There is no need to panic. That is the first rule, he was telling them. The situation is under control, the armed forces are on the alert but at this stage they are taking no further action which would be inappropriate since the Security Forces are already handling every aspect of this matter at every level. Members of the public are advised not to leave their homes without some form of identification.

Several bystanders thrust their hands into their pockets, listened awhile and then furtively moved on: these were the ones who had left their personal documents at home. The civil servant entered a café, sat down and, unusually for someone so abstemious, ordered a strong drink before spreading his newspaper out on the table. A joint declaration had been made by the Ministry of the Interior (MI) and the Ministry of Trade and Industry (MTI), combining and enlarging upon the Formal Statements (FS) issued earlier. Occupying the entire width of the page, the headline reassured readers that 'The situation has not deteriorated within the last 24 hours.' The civil servant muttered nervously to himself: 'And why should it have got worse?' He leafed through the newspaper: minor chaos: news of faults, breakdowns, things disappearing. But not a word about any deaths. A photograph caught the civil servant's attention: it showed a street in which one whole side had disappeared as if no buildings had ever stood there. Apparently taken from the top of another building, the picture showed the labyrinth of foundations, a long strip broken up into rectangular spaces, as in children's games. 'And what about the dead?' he mused, recalling the conversation in the tobacconist's. No mention was made of the dead. Could the Press be concealing the seriousness of the situation? He looked around, turned his eyes up to the ceiling. 'And suppose this building were now to disappear?' he suddenly asked himself. He could feel the cold sweat on his forehead, a knot in his stomach. 'I'm imagining things again. That's always been my trouble.' He summoned the waiter and asked for his bill and, on receiving his change, asked him as he pointed to the newspaper:

—Now then? What do you make of this?

Without even attempting to make the gesture appear natural, he opened his hand. The waiter, whom he had identified earlier as category R, shrugged his shoulders:

—To be frank, I couldn't care less. I think it's a joke.

The civil servant accepted the change in silence and put away his newspaper. Looking quite disdainful, he left and went in search of a telephone box. He dialled the number of the Security Forces (SF) and when someone answered he hastily informed them that in such and such a road, in such and such a café, a waiter had been acting suspiciously. In what way? He told me he couldn't care less and thought the whole situation was a joke. And then he actually said that in his opinion it was no bad thing, and that as far as he was concerned everything could disappear. He didn't? He did. He was not asked for any identification and he offered none: such vague information was unlikely to be rewarded with promotion to category C. But it was a promising start. He emerged from the telephone box and hovered around. Fifteen minutes later a dark-coloured car drew up in front of the café. Two armed men got out and entered the premises. They soon reappeared, bringing the handcuffed waiter with them. The civil servant sighed, turned on his heels and went off whistling.

He felt better out in the fresh air. The natural impulse which had made him telephone and the peace of mind he felt on seeing the waiter being escorted from the café and pushed into the car by the SF caused him some surprise. 'Serving one's city is the duty of every citizen,' he muttered under his breath. 'If everyone were like me, these things would probably never have happened. I pride myself on doing my duty. We must help the Government.' The streets did not appear to have suffered much damage, but there was a general air of neglect throughout the city, as if someone had been going around throwing bits and pieces here and there, like children dropping cake-crumbs: at first, you scarcely notice the mess, then it becomes clear the cake is no longer in a fit state to be served to guests. But there were signs of havoc (or should one say absence?). All the paving on the final stretch of the avenue, an extension of two hundred metres, had vanished. There also appeared to be a burst pipe underground, judging from the enormous crater where the mud swirled and bubbled. Workmen from the Water Department (WD) dug deep gutters around the edges of the crater, exposing the water-pipes. Others consulted the map to find out where the water had to be dammed up and diverted to another ramification of the network. It was a heavily populated area. The civil servant from the DSR went up to take a closer look and began talking to a man standing beside him:

—When did this happen?

The customary handshake revealed that the person he was speaking to belonged to category E.

—Last night. It was quite dreadful, as you can imagine. The street disappeared with everything in it. Even my car.

—Your car?

—All the cars. Everything. Traffic-signals. Pillar-boxes. Lamp-posts. See for yourself. Wiped off the face of the earth.

—But the Government will almost certainly pay compensation. You'll get your car back.

—Of course. I don't doubt it. But has it occurred to you that in this area, according to the statistics provided by the Traffic Wardens, there were between a hundred and eighty and two hundred and twenty cars? And who knows, the same thing may have happened in other streets. Do you think the problem can easily be resolved?

—No, it certainly won't be easy. To pay out compensation for two hundred cars just like that is an expensive business. As someone who works in the DSR, I know what I'm talking about.

The car owner wanted to know his name and they exchanged cards. The water had been cut off at last and the crater barely rippled as the gurgling mud subsided. The civil servant took his leave. This time he really was worried. Any more such incidents and the city would be in a state of chaos.

It was time for lunch. He now found himself in a part of the city he did not know well and rarely frequented, but it should not be difficult to find a modest restaurant within his means. He had thought of returning home to eat, but the situation justified a change of habit. Besides he did not relish the idea of being confined within four walls, inside a building with no front door and where steps were missing. At the very least. Others must have thought the same. The streets were crowded and at times it was impossible to pass. The civil servant settled for a sandwich and a soft drink which he consumed and drank in haste. The restaurants he had come across were practically empty, and he was afraid to enter. 'This is ridiculous,' he thought to himself, unaware that he was qualifying his fear. 'Unless the Government acts with some urgency, this will end in disaster.' Just at that moment a car with a loudspeaker came to a halt in the middle of the street. The amplified voice of a woman reading from a text could be heard blaring from the car: 'May I have your attention. The Government wishes to inform members of the public that it is about to enforce strict laws and sanctions. Some arrests have already been made and the situation is expected to return to complete normality before the day is out. Within the last few hours several cases of things breaking down have been reported, but nothing has disappeared. Members of the public must be on their guard and your full cooperation is essential. Protecting our city is not only the responsibility of the Government and the Armed Forces. Everyone has a duty to protect our city. The Government wishes to express its gratitude to all those citizens who have cooperated so far, but would remind you that the advantages of having so many people guard our streets and squares are outweighed by the disadvantages of this mass presence. The enemy has to be isolated and denied any opportunity of hiding in the crowd. So be on your guard. Our established custom of showing the palms of our hands must now be regarded as a legal obligation. From now on every citizen is authorised to demand, we repeat, to demand of his fellow-citizens that they show the palms of their hands whatever the respective categories. Anyone in category Z can and must demand that a person in category A show his hand. The Government will set an example: this evening on Television, each member of the Government will show the palm of his or her right hand to the nation. Let everyone else do the same. The catch-phrase in our present situation is the following: "On your guard and palms up!'" The four occupants of the car were the first to obey this order. They pressed the palms of their right hands against the windows and drove on, as the woman began repeating her text. Fired with zeal, the civil servant challenged the man who was walking away:

—Show me your hand.

Then turning to a woman:

—Show me your hand.

They showed him their hands and demanded that he should do the same. Within seconds, hundreds of men and women who were just standing there or passing through the street were frantically showing their hands to each other, raising them into the air so that everyone around could bear witness. And soon there were hands everywhere waving frantically in the air, proving their innocence. The practice spread, for there was no more immediate or quicker way of acknowledging and revealing one's identity: people no longer needed to stop, they simply passed each other with outstretched arms, turning their hands out at the wrist, and showing their palm with the letter confirming their category. It was tiresome, but saved time.

Not that there was any shortage of time. The city was still functioning, but very slowly. No one any longer had the courage to use the metro: underpasses inspired terror. Moreover, there was a rumour going round that on one of the lines the power cables were exposed and the first train to go out that morning had electrocuted all the passengers. Perhaps it was not true, or all too true, but there was no lack of detail. On the roads, fewer and fewer buses were running. People dragged themselves through the streets, raised one arm, went on their way, becoming more and more weary, not knowing where to go or rest. In this depressing state of mind, people only had eyes for signs of absence, or for the disruption caused by that same absence. Now and then, truck-loads of soldiers appeared on the scene, as well as a column of tanks, their caterpillar treads squeaking and tearing up great chunks of the road-surface. Overhead, helicopters flew back and forth. People asked each other anxiously: 'Can the situation be so serious? Is there a revolution? Is there likely to be war? But the enemy, where is the enemy?' And unless they had already done so, they raised their arms and showed the palms of their hands.

This also became a favourite game for children: they pounced on the adults like wild beasts, pulled faces, shouting: 'Show me your hand!' And if the exasperated adults, after giving in, demanded to inspect their hands, the children would refuse, stick out their tongue, or show their hands from a distance. Never mind, they were harmless: and the letter on their palms was exactly the same as that of their parents.

The civil servant from the DSR decided to return to his apartment. His bones were aching. Feeling peckish, he began to imagine the little feast he would prepare once he arrived home. The very thought made him even hungrier, he could scarcely wait, the saliva welling up in his mouth. Without thinking, he quickened his pace, and the next minute he was running.

Suddenly he felt himself being grabbed and pushed with force against a wall. Four men were asking him in loud voices why he was running, and shaking him, forced his hand open. Then they had to release him. And he took his revenge by demanding that they should show him the palms of their hands. All of them were in a lower category.

In the apartment block where he lived there appeared to have been no further mishaps. The front door was gone, some steps were missing, but the lift was still working. As he was about to step out on to the landing and confronted the sliding door of the lift, a sudden thought filled him with terror: suppose the lift had broken down or collapsed while making its ascent and he had suddenly crashed to the bottom like those victims he had heard the man in the tobacconist's describe? There and then he decided that until the situation was clarified he would not use the lift, but then he remembered there were steps missing and in all probability it was no longer possible to go down or upstairs. He wavered in the midst of this dilemma, with a concentration that seemed obsessive as he cautiously crossed the landing on tiptoe in the direction of his own front door and realised that the building was plunged into silence except for the odd little creak which was barely audible. Could everyone be out? Were they all down on the street keeping a watchful eye as the Government (G) had requested? Or had they fled? He slowly put one foot on the ground and listened attentively: the sound of coughing on an upper floor put his mind at rest. Opening the door with the utmost care, he went into his apartment. He peered into all the rooms: everything in order. He poked his head inside a kitchen cupboard in the hope that he might miraculously find the jug back in its place. It was not there. He felt quite distressed: this tiny personal loss made the disaster that had befallen the city all the more serious, this collective calamity which he had just witnessed with his own eyes. It occurred to him that just a few minutes ago he had felt the most awful pangs of hunger. Had he suddenly lost his appetite? No, but it had been transformed into a dull pain that caused him to belch as if the walls of his empty stomach were alternately contracting and distending. He made himself a sandwich, which he ate standing in the middle of the kitchen, his eyes slightly glazed, his legs shaking.

The floor was unsteady under his feet. He dragged himself into the bedroom, stretched out fully-clothed on the bed without being aware of the fact and fell into a deep sleep. The rest of the sandwich rolled on to the floor, opening as it fell, his teeth-marks imprinted on one side. Three deafening cracks echoed throughout the room and, as if this were a sign, the room began to twist and sway while retaining all its forms and without any change of features or the relationship between them. The whole building shook from top to bottom. People were shouting on the other floors.

The civil servant slept for four hours without as much as turning. He dreamt that he was standing naked inside an extremely narrow lift which was going up, went through the roof and shot into the air like a rocket, and suddenly vanished leaving him hovering in space for what could have been a tenth of a second, a whole hour, or eternity, and then he began falling down and down, with arms and legs outstretched, observing the city from on high, or its location, for there were no houses or streets in sight, nothing except an empty and totally deserted space. He landed on the ground with a bump and knocked against something with his right hand.

The pain woke him up. The room was already full of shadows as dense as black mist. He sat up in bed. Without looking, he rubbed his right hand with the left, and jumped when he felt something sticky and warm. Even without looking, he could tell it was blood. But how could the tiny wound inflicted by the door at the DSR cause so much bleeding? He switched on the light and examined his hand: the flesh on the back was raw and all the skin covered by the restorative film had disappeared. Still half asleep and shaken by this unexpected setback, he rushed to the bathroom where he kept some first-aid materials in case of emergency. He opened the cupboard and grabbed a bottle. The blood was now dribbling on to the floor and inside the sleeve of his jacket, depending on his movements. This could be a serious haemorrhage. He opened the bottle, dipped in the brush which was in a separate case, and as he was preparing to brush on the biological fluid, he had the distinct feeling that he was about to do something foolish. And suppose the same thing was to happen again? He put the bottle back in its place, spattering blood over everything. There were no bandages in the apartment. Like compresses and adhesives they were hardly used nowadays since this biological restorative fluid had come on to the market. He ran to his room, opened the drawer where he kept his shirts and tore off a long strip of material. Using his teeth, he succeeded in wrapping it tightly round his hand. As he was about to close the drawer, he spotted the rest of the sandwich. He bent down to pick it up, gathered the bits together and, seated on the bed, slowly began munching, not that he was hungry any longer but simply out of a sense of duty he had no wish to question.

Just as he was about to swallow the last mouthful, he noticed a dark patch almost hidden from view by the shadow of a piece of furniture. Intrigued, he went closer, thinking vaguely to himself that once he could afford to buy a carpet all these imperfections in the flooring would disappear. The red patch had been discovered (he would later swear) in a moment of distraction. Stretching out his foot, the civil servant turned it over with the tip of his shoe. He knew what he would find there: on the other side was the film which had been brushed on to the back of his hand, and the red stain was blood, the blood which had formed a lining for the skin attached there. Then he thought it most likely that he would never be able to afford the carpet. He closed the door and made his way to the sitting-room. Outwardly serene and tranquil, he could feel the panic stirring inside him, slowly for the moment, like a heavy armed disc with long spikes capable of tearing him to pieces. He switched on the Television (TV) and, while the set was warming up, he went to the window he had left open since morning. Evening was drawing in. There were lots of people in the street, but seemingly unaware of each other and silent. They were walking about aimlessly, without any apparent destination, extending their arms and showing the palms of their right hands. Viewed from above, in that silence, the spectacle made him want to laugh: arms going up and down, white hands branded with green letters gave a quick wave and then dropped, only to repeat the movement a few paces further on. They were like mental patients driven by some idée fixe as they paraded the grounds of the asylum.

The civil servant went back to watch Television (TV). Round a semi-circular table were seated five panellists of grave demeanour. Even before he could make out a word of what was being said, he noticed that the picture was constantly interrupted as well as the sound. The announcer was speaking:

—gether here specialists . . . ology, industrial safety regulations, biological surgery, pro . . . volved . . . fety . . .

For half-an-hour, the television screen went on flickering, emitting fractured words, the odd phrase that might be complete, although who could be sure. The civil servant just sat there, not all that interested in knowing what they were debating, but because he was in the habit of sitting in front of the Television (TV) and for the moment there was nothing else he could do, if there had ever been a time when he could have done something. He wished the Government (G) would show its hand, not because such a gesture might have any importance, remedy the city's evils or prove some kind of innocence, if that was what it was all about, but just to see all those hands in categories A and B together. Then the picture settled for a few more seconds, the sound became clear, and a voice on the Television (TV) said:

—it seems to be the case that nothing disappears during the day. All one experiences during the day are operational faults, irregularities, breakdowns in general. Whatever has disappeared, has always disappeared during the night.

The person chairing the panel asked:

—What measures do you think should be taken at night?

A member of the panel:

—In my opinion . . .

The picture disappeared, the sound died away until nothing more could be heard. The Television (TV) was no longer working. The Government (G) would not show its hand to the city.

The civil servant returned to his bedroom. As he expected (without knowing why), the patch of restorative film was no longer lying in the same spot. He touched it once more with the tip of his shoe, almost unaware of what he was doing. Then he heard the announcer's voice repeat these words inside his head. 'What measures do you think should be taken during the night?' There were no crackling sounds this time. The whole building was creaking without interruption, as if it were being pulled by two wills in opposite directions. The civil servant tore another strip from his shirt, tied it neatly and securely round his hand, and retrieved from a drawer all the money he possessed. Although it was warm outside, he put on his overcoat: no doubt it would get colder at night and he had no intention of returning home before dawn. 'Everything has disappeared during the night.' He went to the kitchen, made another sandwich which he stuffed into his pocket, ran his eye over the apartment and left.

Once out on the landing, before making his way to the lift, he shouted up the stair-well:

—Anyone at home?

There was no reply. The entire building seemed to be swaying and creaking. 'And suppose the lift isn't working? How am I going to get out of here?' He could see himself jumping from the window of his second-floor apartment on to the street, and gave a deep sigh of relief when the cage door slid back as normal and the light went on. He nervously pressed the button. The lift wavered as if resisting the electrical impulse it was receiving, and then slowly, with laboured jerks, it descended to the ground floor. The door jammed as he tried to open it, leaving barely enough space for him to pass, stretching and squeezing for all he was worth as he edged his way through. The heavy disc of panic was now spinning furiously, turning to vertigo. Suddenly, as if it were giving up the battle or responding to threats, the door surrendered and allowed itself to be opened. The civil servant ran out onto the street. It was already dead of night but the street-lights had still not come on. Shadowy forms passed in silence, fewer people were now raising their hands. But here and there, the odd person still used a cigarette lighter or a pocket torch to see what was happening. The civil servant withdrew into the main entrance of his apartment block. He must get out, he could not bear to feel the building on top of him, but someone was sure to demand that he should show them his hand which was bandaged and bloodstained. People might think the bandage was a ruse, an attempt to conceal the palm of his hand on the pretext that it was injured. He shuddered with fear. But the building was creaking even louder. Something was about to happen.

Forgetting his hand for a second, he dashed out on to the street. He felt an irresistible urge to run, then remembered what had happened to him that afternoon and, with his hand in this state (once more he remembered his hand, and this time there was no forgetting), he realised just how dangerous his situation was. He waited in the dark until there were fewer shadowy figures and fewer lighters and torches going in and out, and then, keeping close to the walls, he took himself off. He reached the end of the street where he lived without anyone questioning him. He gathered his courage. To raise an arm had become absurd in a city where there was no street-lighting, and the inhabitants, weary of their fruitless vigil, gradually stopped demanding to examine the palms of other people's hands.

But the civil servant had not reckoned with the Police (P). On turning a corner which led into a large square, he ran into the patrol. He tried to retreat, but was caught in the act by the beam of a lantern. They ordered him to halt. Were he to try and escape, he would be as good as dead. The patrol advanced on him.

—Show us your hand.

The lantern cast its bright beam on the white bandage.

—What's this?

—I grazed the back of my hand and had to bandage it. The three policemen surrounded him.

—A bandage? What kind of tale is that supposed to be?

How could he explain that the biological liquid had torn away his skin and, at this very moment, was moving around in the darkness of the bedroom? (Moving where?)

—Why didn't you put some biological liquid on the wound? If you really have a wound there, muttered one of the policemen.

—Believe me, there is a wound, but if I remove the bandage now, it will start bleeding again.

—That's enough, we'll do without the chatter. Show us your hand.

The policeman who was nearest dug his finger under the bandage and started tugging with all his might. At first there was no sign of bleeding and then, suddenly, under the harsh glare of the lantern the whole area without skin was covered in blood. The policeman turned up the palm of his hand and the letter came into view.

—On your way.

—Please help me to put the bandage back on, the civil servant pleaded.

Muttering under his breath, 'We're not running a hospital here,' one of the policemen obliged. And then warned him:

—My advice to you is to stay indoors.

Fighting back tears of pain and self-commiseration, he murmured:

—But the apartment block . . .

—That's right, replied the policeman. On your way.

On the other side of the square he could see some lights. He paused. Should he go there and run the risk of constantly bumping into people who would force him to show the palm of his hand? He trembled with pain, fear and anguish. The wound was already bigger. What should he do? Wander through the darkness like so many others, groping his way along, colliding with things? Or return home? The enthusiasm with which he had set out that morning in the role of self-appointed vigilante was fast waning. Whatever he might discover, should he succeed in seeing anything in this darkness, he would not intervene, he would not summon anyone to testify or give assistance. He left the square by a wide road lined with trees on either side where the shadows were deeper. There no one was likely to demand that he should show his hand. People were rushing past but their haste did not imply that they had anywhere to go or knew where they were heading. Walking in haste simply meant, in every sense, to escape.

On both sides of the street, buildings were creaking and crackling. He remembered that at the far end, on a crossing, there was a monument surrounded by benches. He would go and sit there a while, pass the time, perhaps the entire night: he had nowhere to go, what else could he do? No one had anywhere to go. That street, like all the others, was swarming with people. The population seemed to have multiplied. He trembled at the very thought. And it came as no surprise to find that the monument had also disappeared. The benches were still there, some of them occupied. Then the civil servant remembered his wounded hand and hesitated. From the darkness others were emerging and taking up every available space. He could find nowhere to sit.

He had no desire to sit. He turned left, towards a street that had once been narrow but which now had wide, deep openings on both sides, veritable gaps where buildings had once stood. He had the impression that, were it daytime, all those empty spaces would look like perspectives strung together from north to south, from east to west, as far as the city boundaries, if such a term was any longer meaningful. It occurred to him that he could leave the city, go to the outskirts, into the countryside, where there were no buildings to disappear, cars to vanish in their hundreds, things that changed places, and ceased to be there or anywhere else. In the space they once occupied, there was nothing except a void and the occasional dead body. His spirits revived: at least he would escape the nightmare of spending a night like this, amidst invisible threats, going hither and thither. At first light, perhaps he would find some solution to the problem. The Government (G) was sure to investigate the matter. There had been previous cases, although less serious, and they had always found a solution. There was no cause for alarm. Order would be restored to the city. A crisis, a simple crisis and nothing more.

Near the street where he lived some lamps were still lit. This time he did not avoid them: he felt safe, confident, and should anyone question him, he would quietly tell his tale of woe, point out that this was obviously part of the same conspiracy to undermine the security and welfare of the city. It did not prove necessary. No one demanded to see the palm of his hand. The few lit streets were crammed with people. One could only cross the road with the utmost difficulty. And in one street, perched on top of a lorry, a sergeant from the Territorial Army (TA) was reading out a proclamation or warning:

—All members of the public are warned that by order of the Supreme High Command of the Armed Forces the eastern sector of the city will be bombarded from seven a.m. by means of Ground Artillery and Air Attacks as a preliminary measure of retaliation. People who live in the area about to be bombarded have already been evacuated from their homes and are being billeted in government installations with the necessary safeguards. They will be compensated in full for any material losses and the inevitable privations they have suffered. The Government and the Supreme High Command of the Armed Forces can assure all citizens that the plan drawn up for a counter-attack will be carried out to its ultimate consequences. Given the circumstances, and the order of the day, 'On your guard and palms up', having proved to be ineffective, our new slogan will be: 'Look out and attack'.

The civil servant sighed with relief. He would no longer be obliged to show his hand. His self-confidence was restored. The renewed sense of courage he had felt half-an-hour earlier became even stronger. And there and then he made two decisions: he would go back to his apartment, collect his binoculars and take them with him beyond the eastern zone of the city from where he could watch the bombardment. And once the sergeant had finished reading his statement, he joined in the animated conversation that ensued:

—It's an idea.

—Do you think it will work?

—Of course, the Government knows what it's doing. And, as a reprisal, can you think of anything better?

—They'll be taught a lesson this time. Should have happened sooner.

—What have you done to your hand?

—The biological liquid didn't work and only made matters worse.

—I know of a similar case.

—Me too, they told me that it was a disaster for the hospitals.

—I was probably the first case.

—The Government will recompense everyone.

—Good night.

—Good night.

—Good night.

—Good night. Tomorrow is another day.

—Tomorrow is another day. Good night.

The civil servant went off contented. His street was still dark, but this did not worry him. The delicate, imponderable light coming from the stars was enough to show the way, and in the absence of any trees, the darkness was not too dense. He found the road different: several more buildings were missing. But his apartment block was still there. He walked on, most likely more steps had disappeared. But even if the lift should not be working, he would devise some means of reaching the second floor. He wanted his binoculars, he longed for the satisfaction of watching a whole area of the city being bombarded, the eastern sector, as the sergeant had confirmed. He passed between the posts of the missing door and found himself in an empty space. Unlike the building he had seen that morning, all that remained of this one was the façade, like a hollow shell. Looking up, he saw the night sky above and the odd star. He felt a sense of outrage. No fear, only an overwhelming and salutary wrath. Hatred. Blind rage.

On the ground there were white forms, naked bodies. He remembered what he had heard in the tobacconist's that morning: 'Not so much as a ring on their fingers.' He drew closer. Just as he thought, he recognised these corpses: some of them were his neighbours in the same block. They had chosen not to leave the building and now they were dead. Naked. The civil servant placed his hand on a woman's breast: it was still warm. The building had probably disappeared when he had reached the street. Silently or with all that creaking and cracking he had heard everywhere when at home. Had he not stopped to listen to the sergeant and then lingered behind to have a chat, there would probably have been one more corpse here: his own. He looked at the space in front of him where the building had once stood and saw another building further on move, suddenly shrink, like a ragged sheet of dark paper which some invisible fire from the sky was scorching and destroying. In less than a minute, the building had disappeared. And since there was an even greater space beyond, a kind of corridor opened up, and went off in a straight line to the east. 'Even without binoculars', muttered the civil servant, trembling with fear and hatred, 'I must see this.'

The city was immense. For the rest of the night the civil servant headed east. There was no danger of getting lost. On that side, it took longer for the sky to light up. And at seven, already morning, the bombardment would begin. The civil servant felt exhausted but happy. He clenched his left fist, already savouring the terrible fate that was about to befall a quarter of the buildings in the city, to befall everything to be found there, and the OUMIs. He observed that hundreds, thousands of people were walking in the same direction. The same bright idea had occurred to all of them. By five, he had already arrived in the open countryside. Looking back, he could see the city with its irregular outlines, several buildings which appeared to be taller only because the adjacent buildings had disappeared, just as in a sketch of ancient ruins although, strictly speaking, there were no ruins, only a void. Aimed at the city, scores of cannons formed the curve of a circle. So far, not an aeroplane in sight. They would arrive at seven o'clock on the dot, and there was no need for them to arrive sooner. Three hundred metres from the cannons, a cordon of soldiers prevented spectators from getting any closer. The civil servant found himself lost in the crowd. How irritating. He had worn himself out getting there, he had no apartment to return to once the bombardment was over, and now he was going to be deprived of watching the spectacle and enjoying his revenge. He looked around him. People were standing on packing-cases. An excellent idea which had never occurred to him. But behind, perhaps a kilometre away, there was a row of forested hills. Whatever he might lose in terms of distance, he would gain in height. It seemed an idea worth pursuing.

He made his way through the crowd which was already thinning out in that direction, and crossed the open space separating him from the hills. Very few people were heading there. And towards the hill ahead of him, no one. The ashen sky was almost white but the sun still had not risen. The terrain gradually sloped upwards. Between the artillery and the city boundary a row of heavy machine-guns was now being installed. Heaven help any OUMIs that turned up on this side. The civil servant smiled: they were about to get their just deserts. He regretted not being a soldier. How he would have loved to feel in his wrists, yes, even in his wounded hand, the vibrations of a weapon firing, to feel his whole body tremble, not with fear this time, but with anger and blissful revenge. The physical impact on his senses was so intense that he had to pause. He thought of turning back in order to get closer. But realised that he could never be as close as he wished, that in the middle of that crowd he would see precious little, so he carried on. He was now approaching the trees. No one in sight. He sat on the ground with his back to some bushes whose flowers brushed against his shoulders. From all around the city people continued to arrive. No one wanted to miss the spectacle. How many people could be there? Hundreds of thousands. Perhaps the entire city. The countryside was one black stain which was rapidly spreading and already overflowing in the direction of the hills. The civil servant trembled with excitement. After all, this was going to be a resounding victory. It was about seven o'clock. What could have happened to his watch? He shrugged his shoulders: he would have an even better watch, more accurate, of superior quality. Viewed from where he was standing the city was unrecognisable. But everything would be restored in due course. First, punishment.

At that moment he heard voices behind him. The voice of a man and the voice of a woman. He could not make out what they were saying. Perhaps a pair of lovers sexually aroused by the impending bombardment. But the voices sounded tranquil. And suddenly the man said in a clear voice:

—Let's wait a little longer.

And the woman:

—Until the very last minute.

The civil servant could feel his hair stand on end. The OUMIs. He looked anxiously towards the plain. Saw that people were still arriving like a swarm of black ants, and he was determined to win that prize, category C. He quietly circled the thick clump of bushes, then got down, almost crawling behind some trees clustered together. He waited awhile, then got up slowly and spied. The man and woman were naked. He had seen other naked bodies that night, but these were alive. He refused to believe his eyes, heartily wished it was seven o'clock, that the bombardment would commence. Through the branches, he could see people from the city quickly advancing. Perhaps they were already within hearing distance. He called out:

—Help! There are OUMIs here!

Startled, the man and woman turned round and began running towards him. No one else had heard him and there was no time for a second cry for help. He could feel the man's hands tighten round his throat and the woman's hands pressing against his mouth. And before he even had time to look, he already knew that the hands about to strangle him did not bear any letter; they were smooth with nothing except the natural purity of skin. The naked man and woman dragged his body into the woods. More naked men and women appeared and surrounded him. When they moved away, his corpse was lying there stretched out on the ground, naked. Not so much as a ring on his finger, had he ever worn one. Not even a bandage. From the wound on the back of his hand came a tiny trickle of blood which soon dried up.

Between the woods and the city there was no empty space. The entire population had come to witness the great military operation of reprisal. In the distance the drone of aeroplanes approaching. Any clocks that might still be working were about to strike seven or silently mark the hour on the dial. The officer in charge of the artillery was clutching a loudspeaker to give the order to fire. Hundreds of thousands of people, a million, held their breath in suspense. But no shots were fired. For just as the officer was about to shout Fire! the loudspeaker slipped from his hand. Inexplicably, the aeroplanes made a narrow curve and turned back. This was only the opening signal. Total silence spread over the plain. And suddenly the city disappeared. In its place, as far as the eye could see, another multitude of naked men and women emerged from what had once been the city. The cannons disappeared along with all the other weapons, and the soldiers were naked, surrounded by men and women who had earlier worn uniforms and carried weapons. At the centre, the great dark mass of the city's population. But this, too, was almost immediately transformed and multiplied. The plain lit up as the sun rose.

Then from the woods came all the men and women who had been hiding there since the revolution began, since the first OUMI disappeared. And one of them said:

—Now we must rebuild everything.

And a woman replied:

—There was no other remedy since we were those things. Never again will men be treated as things.

The Centaur

The horse came to a halt. His shoeless hooves gripped the round, slippery stones covering the river-bed which was almost dry. Using his hands, the man cautiously pushed back the thorny branches which obstructed his view of the plain. Day was breaking. Far away, where the land rose, first in a gentle slope, for he remembered it being similar to the pass he had descended far north, before suddenly being broken up by a balsatic mountain ridge rising up in a vertical wall, stood some houses which from a distance looked quite small and low, and lights that resembled stars. Along the mountain ridge which cut out the entire horizon from that side, there was a luminous line as if someone had passed a light brushstroke over the peaks and, because still wet, the paint had gradually spread over the slope. The sun would appear from that direction. One false move as he pushed back the branches and the man grazed his hand: he muttered something to himself and put his finger to his lips to suck the blood. The horse retreated, stamping his hooves and swishing his tail over the tall grasses that absorbed the remaining moisture on the river-bank sheltered by overhanging branches forming a screen at that black hour. The river was reduced to a trickle of water running between the stones where the river-bed was deepest and at rare intervals forming puddles wherein fish struggled to survive. The humidity in the atmosphere forecast rain and tempest, perhaps not today but tomorrow, after three suns, or with the next moon. Very slowly the sky began to light up. Time to find a hiding-place in order to rest and sleep.

The horse was thirsty. He approached the stream which seemed quite still beneath the night sky, and as his front hooves met the cool water, he lay down sideways on the ground. Resting one shoulder on the rough sand, the man drank at his leisure despite feeling no thirst. Above the man and the horse, the patch of sky that was still in darkness slowly moved, trailing in its wake the palest light, still tinged with yellow, the first deceptive hint of the crimson and red about to explode over the mountain, as over so many mountains in different places or on a level with the prairie. The horse and man got up. In front stood a dense barrier of trees, with defensive brambles between the trunks. Birds were already chirping on the uppermost branches. The horse crossed the river-bed at an unsteady trot and tried to break through the entangled bushes on the right, but the man preferred an easier passage. With time, and there had been all the time in the world, he had learned how to curb the animal's impatience, sometimes opposing him with an upsurge of violence which clouded his thoughts or perhaps affected that part of his body where the orders coming from his brain clashed with the dark instincts nourished between his flanks where the skin was black; at other times he succumbed, distracted and thinking of other things, things that certainly belonged to this physical world in which he found himself, but not to this age. Fatigue had made the horse nervous: he quivered as if trying to shake off a frenzied gadfly thirsting for blood, and he stamped his hooves restlessly only to tire even more. It would have been unwise to try and force an entry through the entanglement of brambles. There were so many scars on the horse's white coat. One particular scar, which was very old, traced a broad, oblique mark on his rump. When exposed to the blazing sun or when extreme cold made the hairs of his coat stand up, it was as if the flaming blade of a sword were striking that sensitive and vulnerable scar. Although well aware that he would find nothing there except a bigger scar than the others, at such moments the man would twist his torso and look back as if staring into infinity.

A short distance away, downstream, the river-bank narrowed: in all probability there was a lagoon, or perhaps a tributary, just as dry or even more so. It was muddy at the bottom with few stones. Around this pocket as it were, a simple neck of the river that filled and emptied with it, stood tall trees, black beneath the darkness only gradually rising from the earth. If the screen formed by trunks and fallen branches were sufficiently dense, he could pass the day there, completely hidden from sight, until night returned when he could continue on his way. He drew back the cool leaves with his hands and, impelled by the strength of his hocks, he climbed on to the embankment in almost total darkness, concealed by the thick crests of the trees. Then, almost immediately, the ground sloped down again into a ditch which further on would probably run through open countryside. He had found a good spot to rest and sleep. Between the river and the mountain there was arable land, tilled fields, but that deep and narrow ditch showed no signs of being passable. He took a few more steps, now in complete silence. Startled birds were watching. He looked overhead: saw the uppermost tips of the branches bathed in light. The soft light coming from the mountain was now skimming the leafy fringe on high. The birds resumed their chirping. The light descended little by little, a greenish dust changing to pink and white, the subtle and uncertain morning mist. Against the light, the pitch-black trunks of the trees appeared to have only two dimensions as if they had been cut out of what remained of the night and were glued to a luminous transparency that was disappearing into the ditch. The ground was covered with irises. A nice, tranquil refuge where he could spend the day sleeping.

Overcome by the fatigue of centuries and millennia, the horse knelt down. Finding a position to suit both of them was always a difficult operation. The horse usually lay on his side and the man did likewise. But while the horse could spend the entire night in this position without stirring, if the man wanted to avoid getting cramp in his shoulder and all down his side, he had to overcome the resistance of that great inert and slumbering body and make him turn over on to the other side: it was always a disquieting dream. As for sleeping on foot, the horse could, but not the man. And when the hideout was too confined, changing over from one side to another became impossible and the sense of urgency all the greater. It was not a comfortable body. The man could never stretch out on the ground, rest his head on folded arms and remain there studying the ants or grains of earth, or contemplate the whiteness of a tender stalk sprouting from the dark soil. And in order to see the sky, he had to twist his neck, except when the horse reared up on his hind legs, lifting the man on high so that he could lean a little further back; then he certainly got a much better view at the great nocturnal campanula of stars, the horizontal and tumultuous meadow of clouds, or the blue, sunlit sky, the last vestiges of the first creation.

The horse fell asleep at once. With his hooves amongst the irises and his bushy tail spread out on the ground, he lay there breathing heavily at a steady rhythm. Semi-reclined and with his right shoulder pressed up against the wall of the ditch, the man broke off low-lying branches with which to cover himself. While moving he could bear the heat and cold without any discomfort, although not as well as the horse. But when asleep and lying still, he soon began to feel the cold. And so long as the heat of the sun did not become too intense, he could rest at his ease under the shade of the leaves. From this position, he perceived that the trees did not entirely shut out the sky above:

an uneven strip, already a transparent blue, stretched ahead and, crossing it intermittently from one side to the other, or momentarily following in the same direction, birds were flying swiftly through the air. The man slowly closed his eyes. The smell of sap from the broken branches made him feel a little faint. He pulled one of the leafier branches over his face and fell asleep. He never dreamed like other men. Nor did he ever dream as a horse might dream. During their hours of wakefulness, there were few moments of peace or simple conciliation. But the horse's dream, along with that of the man, constituted the centaur's dream.

He was the last survivor of that great and ancient species of men-horses. He had fought in the war against the Lapithae, the first serious defeat suffered by him and his fellow-centaurs. Once they had been defeated, the centaur had taken refuge in mountains whose name he had forgotten. Until that fatal day when, protected in part by the gods, Heracles had decimated his brothers and he alone had escaped because the long, drawn-out battle between Heracles and Nessos had given him time to seek refuge in the forest. And that was the end of the centaurs. But contrary to the claims of historians and mythologists, one centaur survived, this self-same centaur who had seen Heracles crush Nessos to death with one terrible embrace and then drag his corpse along the ground as Hector would later do with the corpse of Achilles, while praising the gods for having overcome and exterminated the prodigious race of the Centaurs. Perhaps remorseful, those same gods then favoured the hidden centaur, blinding Heracles' eyes and mind for who knows what reason.

Each day the centaur dreamt of fighting and vanquishing Heracles. In the centre of the circle of gods who reunited with every dream, he would fight arm to arm, using his croup to dodge any sly move on the enemy's part, and avoid the rope whizzing between his hooves, thus forcing the enemy to fight face to face. His face, arms and trunk perspired as only a man perspires. The horse's body was covered in sweat. This dream recurred for thousands of years and always with the same outcome: he punished Heracles for Nessos' death, summoning all the strength in his limbs and muscles as both man and horse. Set firmly on his four hooves as if they were stakes embedded in the earth, he lifted Heracles into the air and tightened his grip until he could hear the first rib cracking, then another, and finally the spine breaking. Heracles' corpse slipped to the ground like a rag and the gods applauded. There was no prize for the victor. Rising from their gilt thrones, the gods moved away, the circle becoming ever wider until they disappeared into the horizon. From the door where Aphrodite entered the heavens, an enormous star continued to shine.

For thousands of years he roved the earth. For ages, so long as the world itself remained mysterious, he could travel by the light of the sun. As he passed, people came out on to the road-side and threw garlands of flowers over the horse's back or made coronets which they placed on his head. Mothers handed him their children to lift into mid-air so that they might lose any fear of heights. And everywhere there was a secret ceremony: in the middle of a circle of trees representing the gods, impotent men and sterile women passed under the horse's belly: people believed this would promote fertility and restore virility. At certain times of the year they would bring a mare before the centaur and withdraw indoors: but one day, someone who saw the man cover the mare like a horse and then weep like a man was struck blind for committing such a sacrilege. These unions bore no fruit.

Then the world changed. The centaur was banished and persecuted, and forced into hiding. And other creatures too: such as the unicorn, the chimera, the werewolf, men with cloven-hooves, and those ants bigger than foxes but smaller than dogs. For ten human generations, these various outcasts lived together in the wilderness. But after a time, even there they found life impossible and all of them dispersed. Some, like the unicorn, died: the chimerae mated with shrewmice which led to the appearance of bats; werewolves found their way into towns and villages and only on certain nights do they meet their fate; the cloven-footed men also became extinct; and ants grew smaller in size so that nowadays you cannot tell them apart from other small insects. The centaur was now on his own. For thousands of years, as far as the sea would permit, he roamed the entire earth. But on his journeys he would always make a detour whenever he sensed he was getting close to the borders of his native country. Time passed. Eventually there was no longer any land where he could live in safety. He began sleeping during the day and moving on at dusk. Walking and sleeping. Sleeping and walking. For no apparent reason other than the fact that he possessed legs and needed rest. He did not need food. And he only needed sleep in order to dream. And as for water, he drank simply because the water was there.

Thousands of years ought to have been thousands of adventures. Thousands of adventures, however, are too many to equal one truly unforgettable adventure. And that explains why all of them put together did not equal that adventure, already in this last millennium, when in the midst of an arid wilderness he saw a man with lance and coat of armour, astride a scraggy horse charging an army of windmills. He saw the rider being hurled into the air and another man, short and fat and mounted on a donkey, rush to his assistance, shouting his head off. He heard them speak in a language he could not understand and then watched them go off, the thin man badly shaken, the fat one wailing, the scraggy horse limping and the donkey impassive. He thought of going to their assistance but, on taking another look at the windmills, he galloped up to them and, coming to a halt before the first windmill, he decided to avenge the man who had been thrown from his horse. In his native tongue, he called out: 'Even if you had more arms than the giant Briareas, I'll make you pay for this outrage.' All the windmills were left with broken wings and the centaur was pursued to the frontier of a neighbouring country. He crossed desolate fields and reached the sea. Then he turned back.

The centaur, man and beast, is fast asleep. His entire body is at rest. The dream has come and gone, and the horse is now galloping within a day from the distant past, so that the man may see the mountains file past as if they were travelling with him, or he were climbing mountain paths to the summit in order to look down on the sonorous sea and the black scattered islands, the spray exploding around them as if they had just appeared from the depths and were surfacing there in wonder. This is no dream. The smell of brine comes from the open sea. The man takes a deep breath and stretches his arms upwards while the horse excitedly stamps its hooves on protruding marble stones. Already withered, the leaves that were covering the man's face have fallen away. The sun overhead casts a speckled light on the centaur. The face is not that of an old man. Nor that of a young man, needless to say, since we are talking about thousands of years. But his face could be compared with that of an ancient statue: time has eroded it but not to the extent of obliterating the features: simply enough to show they are weather-beaten. A tiny, luminous patch sparkles on his skin, slowly edging towards his mouth, bringing warmth. The man suddenly opens his eyes as a statue might. With undulating movements a snake steals off into the undergrowth. The man raises a hand to his mouth and feels the sun. At that same moment the horse shakes his tail, sweeps it over his croup and chases off a gadfly feeding on the delicate skin of the great scar. The horse rises quickly to his feet accompanied by the man. The day has almost gone and soon the first shadows of night will fall, but there can be no more sleeping. The noise of the sea, which was not a dream, still resounds in the man's ears, not the real noise of the sea but rather that vision of beating waves which his eyes have transformed into those sonorous waves which travel over the waters and climb up rocky gorges all the way to the sun and the blue sky which is also water.

Almost there. The ditch he is following just happens to be there and could lead anywhere, the work of men and a path by which to reach other men. But it heads in a southerly direction and that is what matters. He will advance as far as possible, even in daylight, even with the sun above the entire plain and exposing everything, whether man or beast. Once more he had defeated Heracles in his dream in the presence of all the immortal gods, but once the combat was over, Zeus retreated southwards and only then did the mountains open up, and from their highest peak surmounted by white pillars, he looked down on the islands surrounded by spray. The frontier is nearby and Zeus headed south.

Walking along the deep and narrow ditch, the man can see the countryside from one end to the other. The lands now look abandoned. He no longer knows where the village he had seen at daybreak has disappeared to. The great rocky mountains have become taller or perhaps drawn closer. The horse's hooves sink into the soft earth he is gradually climbing. The man's whole trunk is clearly out of the ditch, the trees space out, and suddenly, once in open countryside, the ditch comes to an end. With a simple movement, the horse makes the final descent, and the centaur appears in full daylight. The sun is to the right and shines directly on to the scar which begins to ache and burn. The man looks back, out of habit. The atmosphere is stuffy and humid. Not that the sea is all that close. This humidity promises rain as does this sharp gust of wind. To the north, clouds are gathering.

The man wavers. For many years he has not dared to travel out in the open unless protected by the darkness of night. But today he feels as excited as the horse. He proceeds through scrubland where the wild flowers give off a strong scent. The plain has come to an end and the ground now rises in humps restricting the horizon or extending it ever more because these elevations are already hills and a screen of mountains looms up ahead. Bushes begin to appear and the centaur begins to feel less vulnerable. He feels thirsty, very thirsty, but there is no sign of water nearby. The man looks behind and sees that one half of the sky is already covered in clouds. The sun lights up the sharp edge of an enormous grey cloud that is steadily approaching.

At this moment, a dog can be heard barking. The horse trembles nervously. The centaur breaks into a gallop between the two hills, but the man does not lose his sense of direction; they must head south. The barking comes nearer, bells can be heard ringing and then a voice speaking to cattle. The centaur stopped to get his bearings, but the echoes misled him and then, suddenly, there is an unexpectedly humid and low-lying stretch of land, a herd of goats appears and in front a large dog. The centaur stopped in his tracks. Several of the ugly scars on his body had been inflicted by dogs. The shepherd cried out in terror and took to his heels as if demented. He began shouting for help: there must be a village nearby. The man ordered the horse to advance. He broke a sturdy branch from a bush in order to chase away a dog which was barking its head off in rage and terror. But fury prevailed: the dog rapidly skirted some boulders and tried to grab the centaur sideways by the belly. The man tried to look back to see where the danger was coming from, but the horse reacted first and, turning quickly on its front hooves, aimed a vicious kick which caught the dog in mid-air. The animal was dashed against some rocks and killed. The centaur had often been forced to defend himself in this way but this time the man felt humiliated. He could feel the strain of all those vibrating muscles in his own body, his ebbing strength, hear the dull thud of his hooves, but he had his back to the battle, played no part in it, a mere spectator.

The sun had disappeared. The heat suddenly abated and there was humidity in the air. The centaur cantered between the hills, still heading south. As he crossed a tiny stream he saw cultivated fields, and when he tried to get his bearings he came up against a wall. There were several houses on one side. Then a shot rang out. He could feel the horse's body twitch as if stung by a swarm of bees. People were shouting and another shot was fired. To the left, splintered branches snapped, but this time no pellets hit him. He stepped back to regain his balance, and with one mighty effort he leapt over the wall. Man and horse, centaur, went flying over, four legs outstretched or drawn in, two arms raised to the sky which was still blue in the distance. More shots rang out, and then a crowd of men began chasing him through the countryside with loud cries and the barking of dogs.

The centaur's body was covered in foam and sweat. He paused for a moment to find the way. The surrounding countryside also became expectant, as if it were listening out. Then the first heavy drops of rain began to fall. But the chase went on. The dogs were following an unfamiliar scent, but that of a deadly enemy: a mixture of man and horse, assassin hooves. The centaur ran faster, and went on running until he perceived that the cries had become different and the dogs were barking out of sheer frustration. He looked back. From a fair distance he saw the men standing there and heard their threats. And the dogs which had darted ahead now returned to their masters. But no one advanced. The centaur had lived long enough to know that this was a frontier, a border. Securing their dogs, the men dared not shoot at him; a single shot was fired, but from so far away that the explosion could not even be heard. He was safe beneath the rain which was pouring down and opening up rapid currents between the stones, safe on this land where he had been born. He continued travelling southwards. The water drenched his white skin, washed away the foam, the blood and sweat, and all the accumulated grime. He was returning much aged, covered in scars, yet immaculate.

Suddenly the rain stopped. The next minute all the clouds had been brushed away and the sun shone directly on to the damp soil, its heat sending up clouds of vapour. The centaur walked slowly as if he were treading powdery snow. He did not know the whereabouts of the sea, but there stood the mountain. He felt strong. He had quenched his thirst with rain, raising his mouth to the sky and taking enormous gulps, with a torrential downpour running down his neck and all the way down his torso, making it glisten. And now he was slowly descending the southern slope of the mountain, skirting the great boulders leaning against each other. The man rested his hands on the highest rocks, where he could feel the soft mosses and rough lichens beneath his fingers, or the sheer roughness of the stone. Below, a valley stretched all the way across which, from a distance, seemed deceptively narrow. Along the valley he could see three villages a fair distance away from each other, the biggest of them in the middle where the road beyond headed south. Cutting across the valley to the right, he would have to pass close to the village. Could he pass there safely? He recalled how he had been pursued, the cries, the shots, the men on the other side of the border. That incomprehensible hatred. This land was his, but who were these men living here? The centaur continued to descend. The day was still far from over. Suffering from exhaustion, the horse trod cautiously, and the man decided it would be just as well to rest before crossing the valley. And after much thought, he decided to wait until dusk: meanwhile he must find some safe spot where he might sleep and recover his strength for the long journey ahead before reaching the sea.

He continued his descent, getting slower and slower. And just as he was finally about to settle down between two boulders, he saw the black entrance to a cave, high enough to allow the man and horse to enter. Using his arms and stepping gingerly with tender hooves on those hard stones, he entered the cave. It was not very deep, but there was enough room inside to move at one's ease. Supporting his forearms against the rocky surface of the wall, the man was able to rest his head. He was breathing deeply, trying to resist rather than accompany the horse's laboured panting. The sweat was pouring down his face. Then the horse pulled in his front hooves and allowed himself to slump to the ground which was covered with sand. Lying down or slightly raised as was his wont, the man could see nothing of the valley. The mouth of the cave only opened to the blue sky. Somewhere deep inside, water was dripping at long, regular intervals, producing an echo as if from a well. A profound peace filled the cave. Stretching one arm behind him, the man passed his hand over the horse's coat, his own skin transformed, or skin which had transformed into him. The horse quivered with pleasure, all his muscles distended, and sleep took possession of his great body. The man released his hands allowing it to slip on to the dry sand.

The setting sun began to light up the cave. The centaur dreamt neither of Heracles nor of the gods seated in a circle. Nor were there any more visions of mountains facing the sea, of islands sending up spray, or of that infinite and sonorous expanse of water. Nothing but a dull, dark wall or simply colourless and insurmountable. Meanwhile, the sun penetrated to the bottom of the cave causing all the rock crystals to sparkle, and transforming each drop of water into a crimson pearl that had become detached from the roof after swelling to an incredible size, and then traced a blazing trail three metres long before sinking into a tiny pool already plunged into darkness. The centaur was asleep. The blue sky faded, the space was flooded by the myriad of colours of the forge and evening descended slowly, dragging in the night like some weary body about to fall asleep in its turn. Cast into darkness, the cave had become enormous and the drops of water fell like round stones on to the rim of a bell. It was already darkest night when the moon appeared.

The man woke up. He felt the anguish of not having dreamt. For the first time in thousands of years he had not had a dream. Had it abandoned him the moment he had returned to the land of his birth? Why? Some omen? What oracle could tell? The horse, more remote, was still asleep but stirring restlessly. From time to time he would move his hind legs as if he were galloping in dreams, not his, for he had no brain, or only on loan, but stirred by the willpower in his muscles. Resting his hand on a protruding stone, the man raised his trunk and, as if sleep-walking, the horse followed him effortlessly, with flowing movements which seemed weightless. And the centaur emerged into the night.

The moon cast its light over the entire valley. So much light that it could not possibly be coming from that simple little moon on earth, Selene, silent and spectral, but the light of all the moons elevated above an infinite succession of nights where other suns and lands without these or any other names rotate and shine. The centaur took a deep breath through the man's nostrils: the air was soft, as if it were passing through the filter of human skin, and it had the smell of damp soil that was slowly drying out between the labyrinthine embrace of roots securing the world. He descended into the valley by an easy, almost tranquil route, his four equine limbs harmoniously swaying, swinging his two male arms, moving step by step, without disturbing a stone or risking any more cuts on some sharp ridge. And so he finally reached the valley as if this journey were part of the dream he had been deprived of while asleep. Ahead there was a wide river. On the other bank, slightly to the left, stood the largest of the villages on the southern route. The centaur advanced out into the open, followed by that singular shadow without equal in this world. He cantered through the cultivated fields, choosing beaten paths to avoid trampling the plants. Between the strip of cultivated land and the river there were scattered trees and signs of cattle. Picking up their scent, the horse became restless, but the centaur went on heading for the river. He cautiously entered the water, using his hooves to feel his way. The water became deeper until it came up to the man's chest. In the middle of the river, beneath the moonlight, another flowing river, anyone watching there would have seen a man crossing the ford with upraised arms, his arms, shoulders and head those of a man, and with hair instead of a mane.

Concealed in the water walked a horse. Roused by the moonlight, fishes swam around him and pecked his legs.

The man's entire torso emerged from the water, then the horse appeared, and the centaur mounted the river-bank. He passed underneath some trees and on the threshold of the plain stopped to get his bearings. He remembered how they had pursued him on the other side of the mountain, he recalled the dogs and shots, the men and their cries, and he felt afraid. He now wished the night were darker and would have preferred to walk under a storm like that of the previous day which forced the dogs to seek shelter and sent people scurrying indoors. The man thought everyone in those parts must already know of the centaur's existence for the news must surely have travelled across the border. He realised he could not cross the countryside in a straight line in broad daylight and slowly began following the river protected by the shade of the trees. Perhaps ahead he might find more favourable terrain where the valley narrowed and ended up compressed between two high hills. He continued to think about the sea, about the white pillars, and closing his eyes he could see once more the trail left by Zeus when he headed south.

Suddenly, he heard the lapping of water. He remained still and listened. The noise came back, died away, then returned. On the ground covered with couch grass, the horse's steps became so muffled that they could not be heard amidst the manifold murmurings of tepid night and moonlight. The man pushed back the branches and looked towards the river. There was clothing lying on the river-bank. Someone was bathing. He pushed the branches further back and saw a woman. She emerged from the water completely naked and her white body shone beneath the moonlight. The centaur had seen women many times before, but never like this, in this river and with this moon. On other occasions he had seen swaying breasts and hips, that dark spot in the centre of their body. On other occasions he had seen tresses falling over shoulders and hands tossing them back, such a familiar gesture. But his only contact with the world of women was that which might please the horse, perhaps even the centaur, but not the man. And it was the man who looked and saw the woman retrieve her clothes; it was the man who pushed through those branches, trotted up to her and, as she screamed, lifted her into his arms.

This, too, he had done on several occasions, but they were so few over thousands of years. A futile action, merely frightening, an act which could have resulted in madness and perhaps did. But this was his land and the first woman he had seen there. The centaur ran alongside the trees, and the man knew that further ahead he would put the woman down on the ground, he frustrated, she terrified, the woman intact, he only half-man. Now a broad path came close to the trees and ahead there was a curve in the river. The woman was no longer screaming, simply sobbing and trembling. And at that moment they heard other cries. On rounding the bend, the centaur came to a halt before a small group of low houses concealed by trees. People were gathered outside. The man pressed the woman to his chest.

He could feel her firm breasts, her pubes at the spot where his human body disappeared and became the horse's pectorals. Some people fled, others threw themselves forward, while others ran into their houses and reappeared carrying rifles. The horse got up on his hind legs and reared into the air. Terrified, the woman let out another scream. Someone fired a shot into the air. The man realised the woman was protecting him. Then the centaur headed for the open countryside, avoiding any trees that might impede his movements, and, still clutching the woman in his arms, he skirted the houses and galloped off across the open fields in the direction of the two hills. He could hear shouting coming from behind. Perhaps they had decided to pursue him on horseback, but no horse could compete with the centaur, as had been demonstrated in thousands of years of constant flight. The man looked behind: the persecutors were still some way off, some considerable way off. Then, gripping the woman under her arms, he gazed at her whole body stripped naked under the moonlight and said to her in his former tongue, in the language of the forests, of honeycombs, of the white columns of the sonorous sea, of laughter on the mountains:

—Don't hate me.

He then put her down gently on the ground. But the woman did not escape. From her lips came words the man was capable of understanding:

—You're a centaur. You exist. She placed her hands on his chest. The horse's legs trembled. Then the woman lay down and said:

—Cover me.

The man saw her from above, stretched out in the form of a cross. For a moment, the horse's shadow covered the woman. Nothing more. Then the centaur moved sideways and broke into a gallop, while the man began shouting and clenching his fists at the sky and the moon. When his pursuers finally reached the woman, she had not stirred. And when they carried her off wrapped in a blanket, the men carrying her could hear her weep.

That night, the whole country learned of the centaur's existence. What at first had been treated as some rumour from across the border to keep them amused, now had reliable witnesses, amongst them a woman who was trembling and weeping. While the centaur was crossing this other mountain, people came from the nearby villages and towns, with nets and ropes, and even with firearms, but only to scare him off. He must be captured alive, they said. The army was also put on the alert. They were waiting for daylight before sending up helicopters to search the entire region. The centaur kept under cover, but could hear the dogs barking at frequent intervals, and in the waning moonlight even caught sight of men scouring the mountains. The centaur travelled all night in a southerly direction. And when the sun came up, the centaur was standing on top of a mountain from where he could view the sea. Way in the distance, nothing but the sea, not an island in sight, and the sound of a breeze which smelt of pines, not the lashing of waves or the pungent odour of brine. The world appeared to be a wilderness waiting to be populated.

It was not a wilderness. Suddenly a shot rang out. And then, forming a wide circle, men emerged from behind the stones, making a great din, yet unable to hide their fear as they advanced with nets and ropes, nooses and staffs. The horse reared into the air, shook its front hooves and swung round in a frenzy to face his enemies. The man tried to retreat. Both of them struggled, behind and in front. And the horse's hooves slipped on the edge of the steep slope, they scrambled anxiously seeking some support, the man's hands, too, but the cumbersome body lost its footing and fell into the abyss. Twenty metres below, a jutting edge of rock, inclined at just the right angle, polished by thousands of years of cold and heat, sun and rain, and hewn by wind and snow, cut through the centaur's body at the very spot where the man's torso became that of the horse. The fall ended there. At long last the man lay stretched out on his back and looking up at the sky. An ever deepening sea overhead, a sea with tiny, motionless clouds that were islands, and immortal life. The man turned his head from one side to the other: nothing but endless sea, an interminable sky. Then he looked at his body. It was bleeding. Half a man. A man. And he saw the gods approaching. It was time to die.

Revenge

The boy was coming from the river. Barefoot, with his trousers rolled up above his knees, his legs covered in mud. He was wearing a red shirt, open in front where the first hairs of puberty on his chest were beginning to blacken. He had dark hair, damp with the sweat that was trickling down his slender neck. He was bent slightly forward under the weight of the long oars, from which were hanging green strands of waterweeds still dripping. The boat kept swaying in the murky water, and nearby, as if spying, the globulous eyes of a frog suddenly appeared. Then the frog moved suddenly and disappeared. A minute later the surface of the river was smooth and tranquil and shining like the boy's eyes. The exhalation of the mud released slow, flaccid bubbles of gas which were swept away by the current. In the oppressive heat of the afternoon, the tall poplars swayed gently, and, in a flurry, like a flower suddenly blossoming in mid-air, a blue bird flew past, skimming the water. The boy raised his head. On the other side of the river, a girl was watching him without moving. The boy raised his free hand and his entire body traced out some inaudible word. The river flowed slowly.

The boy climbed the slope without looking back. The grass ended right there. Above and beyond, the sun burnt the clods of untilled soil and ashen olive-groves. In the distance, the atmosphere trembled.

It was a one-storeyed house, squat, whitewashed with a border painted bright yellow. A stark wall without windows, a door with an open peephole. Inside, the earthen floor was cool underfoot. The boy rested his oars and wiped away the perspiration with his forearm. He remained still, listening to his heartbeat, the sweat slowly resurfacing on his skin. He remained there for several minutes, oblivious to the sounds coming from behind the house and which suddenly turned into a deafening outburst of squealing: the protestations of an imprisoned pig. When he finally began to stir, the animal's cry, now wounded and outraged, deafened him. Other cries followed, piercing and wrathful, a desperate plea, a cry expecting no help.

He ran to the yard, but did not cross the threshold. Two men and a woman were holding down the pig. Another man, with a knife covered in blood, was making a vertical slit in the scrotum. Glistening on the straw was a squashed crimson ovule. The pig was trembling all over, squeals coming from the jaws secured with a rope. The wound opened up, the testis appeared, milky and streaked with blood, the man inserted his fingers into the opening, pulled, twisted and plucked inside.

The woman's face twitched and turned pale. They untied the pig, removed the cord round its snout, and one of the men bent down and grabbed the two thick, soft testicles. Perplexed, the animal swerved round and, gasping for breath, stood there with its head lowered. Then the man threw the testicles to the ground. The pig caught them in its mouth, avidly chewed and swallowed. The woman said something and the men shrugged their shoulders. One of them started laughing. And at that moment they saw the boy in the doorway. Taken unawares, they fell silent and, at a loss as to what they should do, they began staring at the animal which had lain down on the straw, breathing heavily, its lips stained with its own blood.

The boy went back inside. He filled a mug and drank, allowing the water to trickle down the corners of his mouth, then down his neck on to the hairs on his chest which seemed darker. As he drank, he stared outside at those two red stains on the straw. Then he stepped wearily out of the house, crossed the olive-grove once more beneath the scorching sun. The dust burned his feet but, pretending not to notice, he walked on tiptoe to avoid that burning sensation. The same cicada was screeching on a lower key. Then down the slope, the grass smelling of warm sap, the inebriating coolness beneath the branches, the mud getting between his toes until it covered them.

The boy remained there, watching the river. Settled on the sprouting mosses, a frog as brown as the previous one, with round eyes under bulging arches, appeared to be lying in wait.

The white skin of its gullet was palpitating. Its closed mouth creased scornfully. Time passed and neither the frog nor the boy moved. Then, averting his eyes with difficulty as if fleeing some evil spell, he saw the girl reappear on the other side of the river, amidst the lower branches of the willows. And once again, silent and unexpected, a blue streak passed over the water.

Slowly the boy removed his shirt. Slowly he finished undressing and it was only when he no longer had any clothes on that his nakedness was slowly revealed. As if he were healing his own blindness. The girl was watching from afar. Then, with the same slow gestures, she removed her dress and everything else she was wearing. Naked against the green backcloth of trees.

The boy again looked at the river. Silence descended on the liquid skin of that interminable body. Circles widened and disappeared on the calm surface, marking the spot where the frog had plunged in. Then the boy got into the water and swam to the other bank as the white, naked form of the girl withdrew into the shadow of the branches.

Acknowledgements

Harper Collins for permission
— 'Reflux' and 'Revenge' in: *Frontiers* (*Leopard III*), London: Harvill, 1994, pp. 293–304 and 305–7.

The Trustees of Oklahoma State University for permission
— 'Embargo' in: *Cimarron Review*, 110 (1995), pp. 10–19.

Own copyright
— 'The Centaur' in: *Passport to Portugal* (A Passport Anthology, No. 8), London: Serpent's Tail, 1994, pp. 5–19; and *The Literary Review*, 38 (1995), 4, pp. 543–556.
— 'The Chair' in: *Passport to Portugal* (A Passport Anthology, No. 8), London: Serpent's Tail, 1994, pp. 136–151.
— 'Things' in: *The Translator's Dialogue: Giovanni Pontiero* (eds. Pilar Orero and Juan C. Sager), Amsterdam: John Benjamins, 1997, pp. 187–245.

On the Typeface

This book is set in Electra, a typeface designed by William Addison Dwiggins for use on Linotype typesetting machines in 1935. Dwiggins, a mildly eccentric book designer, illustrator, calligrapher and creator of marionettes, is credited with complained about the term 'graphic design'.

Dwiggins's foray into type design began with a challenge from the Mergenthaler Linotype Company, after he had complained about the dearth of usable san serifs. Electra was Dwiggins's first type design for book setting and would be one of his most enduring.

Dwiggins sought to create a typeface that reflected the modern environment. Electra was based on his own calligraphic hand. Its unbracketed serifs, flat arches, and open counters make for a face mild in pretence but alive in personality.